For Elia,

Thank you for
your support
ot my writing!
Jane Z.
March 2012

Talking Waters

A young adult novel by

Jane Zimmermann

Talking Waters is a work of fiction.

Visit **www.patchespublishing.com** for more information or to order additional copies.

Table of Contents

Chapter 1

Summer Plans

Audrey paused in the doorway to Erin's room, eager to share her good news, but reluctant to interrupt her friend who was so intent on studying. She stood silently, waiting for the right moment to say something, but her impulsive little dog Patches was not that patient. The energetic Jack Russell bounded into the room and announced their arrival by circling at the girl's feet. Erin's pretty face lit up and her blue eyes looked genuinely happy when she saw her guests.

"Bonjour Audrey! Es-tu fini avec notre travail? I am so tired of homework, even French!" Erin sighed. "Je suis fatiguée! I can't wait for school to end this year." The slight blonde girl got up from her desk to greet the little dog and her best friend.

"Patches can't wait either," Audrey said with a grin on her face. "She's excited about spending the summer at Lake Bonita."

It took a second for the news to register with Erin, who was obviously not happy when she understood what her friend was saying. "You're going away for the summer?" she asked seriously, already thinking about how lonely she would be if she had to spend the whole summer without Audrey.

"Yes – and so are you!" Audrey blurted out, enjoying the confused look on Erin's face.

John Harris loved to hear his daughter's laughter drifting downstairs to his office while he wrote. The distant sound of teenage voices in the house and the deep steady breathing of the big brown dog at his feet created a perfect background for the author to work. Sadie, the family Lab, lifted her head and looked around from time to time, but for the most part she let the man at the desk do all the work. His current book was a history of their town Dunellon, which had been inspired by his son's passion for local history. As a matter of fact, with Erin and Audrey's help, Dakota had uncovered a lot more than just artifacts in their sleepy little town.

Erin's father liked Audrey and was grateful that she had become such good friends with his children. The two girls, both 14, had met when Audrey and her parents moved in down the street just before school started last fall. It had been difficult for sophisticated Audrey Conroy to move from Washington, DC, to the quiet country town of Dunellon, but making new friends had made the transition easier for her. In turn, Audrey's friendship had helped Erin and Dakota through the painful trauma of losing their mother, who had died in a plane crash shortly before Audrey moved to Dunellon.

Sadie snored loudly, jolting the writer back to his work. Just as he was attempting to describe the thrill of discovering an archeological relic, his son burst into the room. As usual, Dakota's blue eyes were lit with excitement, lending a sense of urgency to everything he said and did. Mr. Harris wished he had just a fraction of the boy's energy.

"Dad! Audrey and Erin told me about the house at Lake Bonita! Did you know that's right by Monticello - Thomas Jefferson's home? I bet we'll find a ton of stuff to explore out there!" He paused for a quick breath, then asked with uncertainty, "It's alright with you if we go, isn't it? Audrey's Dad said he already talked to you and he wants us to go because he knows Audrey wouldn't be happy there without us. You know as well as I do it would be impossible to separate Erin and Audrey." The last sentence was spoken with an adult air of logic.

"Of course it's OK, son," said the man warmly, suddenly realizing how quickly his children were growing up, "but there are still some details we have to work out. It's a generous invitation from the Conroys - maybe too generous for my liking - and we definitely have to discuss the parental supervision. There's no way we're leaving the three of you out there alone!"

"But Dad, I'll be 17 this summer!" insisted Dakota, as if that explained everything.

"My point exactly!" answered his father with a resounding laugh. "Don't worry, we'll make it work," he reassured his son. "What will you do with your lawn jobs if you go away for the summer? That's something you need to think about. Now don't you have some homework to do? I have a book to write." He ushered his son out of the office, sat back down with a smile on his face and started typing.

Chapter 2

The Lake House

Alecia Conroy stood in the middle of the vast living room with her hands on her hips and an upset look on her face. "This place is filthy," she said quietly. Her voice was so packed with emotion that everybody in the room fell silent.

The day had not started out like that. In fact, it had started out like an adventure. Everyone had been eager to see the lake house where they would be spending the summer and the three hour drive had been fun. Dakota hadn't stopped talking about the history of the area, Erin and Audrey were thrilled about the prospect of swimming every day, and Mr. and Mrs. Conroy hoped to spend the summer playing tennis and reading, like being at a resort. Patches had been thrilled just to be in the car with everybody. Mr. Harris had stayed home, claiming that he and Sadie had a lot of work to do.

The little group of travellers had been very upbeat. Mrs. Conroy had even said she would try to manage without her housekeeper at the lake house for the entire summer. Nora was a fixture in the Conroy household, but she had balked at the idea of being uprooted from her kitchen to some "camp." Everybody knew if Audrey spent the summer at the "camp," it was doubtful Nora would enjoy being at home - the housekeeper adored the girl.

Erin and Audrey and Dakota promised Mrs. Conroy they would help with the housekeeping over the summer, but their promises didn't seem to reassure the woman. She knew from experience how easily her daughter forgot even the most sincere promise, especially when it came to chores as tedious as laundry and dishes. With a lake right outside their door, Mrs. Conroy knew where the teens would be. She would have to look for some local help if she didn't want to handle the bulk of the housework on her own.

Mr. Conroy had arranged to meet the realtor at a country store near the lake and she was late, so they had lunch at the little deli inside the store while they waited. The adults were finishing their sandwiches and the teens were eyeing the ice cream case in the back when a middle-aged woman rushed in, totally flustered and disheveled. She looked like an eccentric witch from one of the Harry Potter movies. When the woman held out a big bunch of keys to Mr. Conroy, the girls exchanged amused glances.

"You must be Alan Conroy!" she exclaimed breathlessly. "Sorry, I'm so late. I have a closing that is not going smoothly and my assistant is out sick today. I just ran out here to give you the keys. Hi, everybody." The woman looked around the table and smiled at the faces watching her curiously. "I'm so glad you were able to drive out here today to see the house. Do you think you can find it by yourself? I hope you don't mind if I don't go with you," she said apologetically. "I really am sorry. You can take as long as you like and just bring the keys back here when you're done. My office is across the street and that girl back there with the ice cream is my daughter Heather." This time the woman actually paused long enough to look up and smile broadly at her daughter before continuing her monologue. The pretty young girl at the ice cream counter smiled and waved back at her mother.

"I imagine we can find the house on our own," said Mr. Conroy with his usual confidence. "I'll just plug the address into my GPS and let Dakota drive." Dakota's eyes widened when he heard that, but he wasn't sure if Mr. Conroy was serious or not. "We'll bring the keys back here when we're done and I'll give you a call during the week to let you know what we decide."

"If we do rent the house, it won't be for another month," added Mrs. Conroy. "We're going to wait until school gets out."

"Of course, of course. Thank you all so much!" The realtor was visibly relieved. She turned to Mr. Conroy before rushing out the door and handed him her card. "Call my cell phone if you need anything and I'll get back to you as soon as I get out of this closing. You guys are going to love it here! Bye Heather!" the last words to her daughter were thrown over her shoulder as the frenzied woman rushed out the door.

"How about an ice cream cone for the road?" Mr. Conroy asked. He quickly qualified the offer, "for passengers only.

Dakota, would you rather drive or eat ice cream? The choice is yours."

It was hard to say what influenced Dakota's decision more - the ice cream itself or the pretty girl serving it, but the end result was three teenagers with ice cream cones in the back and Mr. and Mrs. Conroy with Patches in the front. Following his GPS directions around the lake, Mr. Conroy stopped at the end of a desolate, totally overgrown driveway.

He turned the ignition off and there was a noticeable silence in the car. "Well, I think we're here," he said with hesitation in his voice. "Let me just take a look down this little road to make sure we're in the right place. Sit tight for a minute." From her perch on Mrs. Conroy's lap, Patches watched the man's every move as he climbed out of the car and disappeared down the jungle-like driveway.

Mr. Conroy returned to the car almost immediately, his confident smile back on his face. "Wait until you see this view," he said quietly as he navigated the big BMW through the little tunnel of a driveway formed by overhanging tree limbs and overgrown shrubs. He winced when he heard branches scraping the sides of his car, but he didn't say a word. He came to a stop in front of a rambling wooden structure perched on a very private lot overlooking the lake. Old dried leaves were everywhere, burying the driveway, completely covering the yard, and even knee-deep on the decks. The house was in an obvious state of disrepair, but there was something appealing about it – appealing enough so that Mrs. Conroy kept her comments to herself at first, much to the surprise of everybody with her. This was definitely not what she had expected. The teens exchanged glances, quietly waiting for an outburst from Audrey's mother which didn't come.

Mr. and Mrs. Conroy and Patches got out first, wading through a sea of leaves onto the leaf-filled deck and up to the front door. The teens piled out of the back seat and followed the adults through the dilapidated front door into a huge living room. Mr. Conroy gently turned his wife's shoulders so that she stood facing an amazing wall of windows overlooking the lake. "Look out the window, sweetheart. That view is what we came here for!"

"Even the windows are filthy!" snapped Mrs. Conroy. The outburst everyone had been anticipating finally arrived, and in no uncertain terms, the woman began to express her displeasure with the state of the house. Erin, Audrey and Dakota escaped outside as quickly as possible to admire the incredible view from the leaf-filled wrap-around deck. Sunlight filtered through the tops of the huge trees surrounding the house and the lake sparkled below them. It was mesmerizing.

Patches followed the teens and immediately took off to explore a narrow path leading down to a rickety-looking dock which held a couple of grungy plastic chairs and two brightly colored kayaks. Dakota was thrilled to see the kayaks on what he hoped was their dock. Patches checked out the kayaks and came bounding back up the path to the deck.

Audrey's parents joined the teens outside after a few minutes. Mr. Conroy had somehow managed to calm his wife, and almost against her will, Mrs. Conroy admitted the view was beautiful. Of course, that didn't mean she was happy.

"Alan, do you think this deck is safe?" she asked in an agitated voice. "It feels like it's about to collapse right beneath our feet. What's up with this house? It's a mess!"

"I'll talk to the realtor," Mr. Conroy promised his wife. "We'll get someone in here to clean it up and do some yard work and we'll have the deck inspected before summer starts. Remember, it's just a rental. We're not buying it and we're not going to live here forever. I think it's great for a summer camp and I bet the kids will have a blast here - and you will too, if you just relax," he said with finality. Something in the tone of his voice made it clear he did not wish to discuss it any more. Everybody was glad when Dakota changed the subject.

"Check out the kayaks!" said the boy excitedly. "Is that our dock? Mr. Conroy, can we use them this summer? Is it OK if we go down there?" Dakota's enthusiasm eased the tension and put a smile on everybody's face.

"Let's all go check out the dock — it has to be in better shape than that living room," said Mrs. Conroy in a more positive tone and she started to lead the little group down the path to the dock. "I definitely need a break before we go back inside to explore the rest of that house." There was more than a hint of sarcasm in her voice, but she was smiling.

The path was steeper than it looked, and when Mrs. Conroy leaned on her husband's arm for support, Erin had an intense flash of sadness. Watching her friend's parents together reminded Erin of how her family used to be. It had been a bit over a year since she lost her mother and she wondered if she would ever stop missing her. She knew Dakota felt the same way even though they seldom talked about it. Erin stood on the little dock with her brother and the Conroy family and suddenly realized her father must be incredibly lonely. She needed to remember that. Her all-too serious thoughts were interrupted by Audrey's shout.

"Look – a bald eagle!" The girl's slender arm pointed up into the sky and everyone turned to look at the magnificent bird gliding directly over their heads. They stood silently, gazing back and forth from the soaring eagle to the beautiful view of the lake in front of them.

Patches raced from the top of the path back to the bottom over and over again, obviously enjoying the exercise. The peaceful setting had a calming effect on Mrs. Conroy and this time she remained silent as they waded through the leaves on the way up to the house.

Once they were back inside, Erin and Audrey exchanged quiet grins with Mr. Conroy before they left him with his wife in the kitchen. The big man was patiently taking notes while his wife dictated everything that needed to be fixed or cleaned or replaced before they moved into the house for the summer. "The bedroom on the main floor is ours," Mrs. Conroy called after the girls. "You two can choose either upstairs or down. If I were you, I'd claim the upstairs rooms before Dakota does!" The boy had already gone back outside, probably on one of his historical treasure hunts.

The girls did not need any more encouragement. They bolted up the stairs with Patches on their heels and soon their "oooh's" and "aaaah's" and giggles could be heard echoing down into the living room. The two bedrooms and small bath upstairs were joined by a long hallway (yet another race track for Patches) which was open to the living room. Standing in the middle of the hall, the girls had a full view of the wall of windows overlooking the deck and the trees and the lake below. It was beautiful.

Each bedroom had a small rickety balcony which proved to be irresistible to the girls. They ventured cautiously out onto one of the wobbly structures to admire the view, which was incredible. A wide expanse of the lake lay before them on one side of the house and on the other side it looked like there was a park or a nature preserve right next door. The trees were thick there, but they could see a small path leading into the woods that looked inviting, but also a bit eerie.

Audrey slowly turned away from the panoramic view. "Mom's right," she said. "Let's take these bedrooms. I don't even need to see the downstairs. I love the light and the views from up here." Erin nodded, agreeing without question or comment. The two girls were totally different in appearance and personality, but there was an unmistakable bond between them. Erin's shy, reserved personality matched her slender, blonde, blue-eyed appearance, and Audrey's outgoing, cheerleader character matched the long legs and stunning good looks she had inherited from her mother. Mrs. Conroy and Audrey both had soft brown eyes, silky brown hair, high cheekbones and figures like models.

"There's Cody!" Audrey nudged her friend's arm and leaned over the rickety railing of the deck to point at the figure far below them. Audrey yelled down to Dakota, who was picking something up from the ground, and both girls laughed as he looked around to see where the voice had come from. When he finally figured out where they were, the boy waved excitedly for them to join him in the yard. Erin rolled her eyes at Audrey as they left the balcony to go back inside, pretty certain her brother had found an artifact or something that only he considered a treasure – Dakota was like a magnet for that kind of stuff and they were curious to see what he had found this time. The two girlfriends raced back down the steps, almost in unison, with the little dog running circles around them. Patches got there first.

Chapter 3

Change of Plans

Dakota's enthusiasm about the lake house grew exponentially when he discovered a pottery shard in the yard. There were letters on the shard which he insisted were part of the word *coffee,* so he immediately decided to take it to Monticello when he started working there. Talk about positive thinking – he hadn't even had a job interview yet. At any rate, excitement about spending the summer at the lake carried the teens through the last four weeks of school and the grueling tests at the end of the year. None of them actually breezed through finals, but Erin and Audrey did well because they studied hard, and Dakota somehow managed to get by, as usual. The teachers and the students all loved the eager, enthusiastic boy.

Dakota had his heart set on really getting to know Thomas Jefferson over the summer. He had already started looking into a part-time job at Monticello, Jefferson's home. But first he had some arrangements to make at home. He had been mowing lawns and doing yard work around Dunellon for years and he couldn't let his loyal customers down for an entire summer. In the end, the boy's personality and great work history paid off. His customers were happy the boy had the opportunity to get away for the summer and they promised to hire him back in the fall.

Once again, Erin was amazed at how things seemed to fall in place for her brother with little or no effort on his part. "I can't believe everything is so easy for Dakota," she confided to Audrey with more than a hint of jealousy in her voice. "He hardly studies at all and he passes everything. His teachers love him and he can do anything he wants with his customers."

"But you have to admit, he does deserve it in a certain way," Audrey defended her friend's brother. "He's so good-natured and always doing stuff for other people. I know he would do anything to help either one of us."

"Yeah, especially if it involved homemade cookies," laughed Erin as she pointed towards Audrey's house. Dakota was standing on the front porch talking to Nora, the Conroy's housekeeper, with a plate of rapidly vanishing cookies between them. The girls picked up their pace, eager to share in the goodies.

Nora's face lit up when she saw the girls. She adored Audrey and was pleased that her young charge had friends like Erin and Dakota.

"Don't worry, there are plenty more where these came from," said Nora, as if reading their minds. "I wouldn't let you down on the last day of school. Now come on in and get some milk. There's another batch of cookies in the oven."

None of the teens waited for a second invitation. Patches came tearing out to greet them as if she understood what a great feeling it was to be done with school and have the whole summer ahead of her. Audrey and Erin greeted the energetic little dog before they went in to sit at the counter in Nora's kitchen and talk about their exams and the lake house and Monticello and cookies and dogs and... The realization that summer had finally arrived intensified with every cookie.

"Nora, I wish you would change your mind and come to the lake house with us," Audrey pleaded. "It'll be so weird without you." Erin and Dakota nodded their agreement, trying to encourage the housekeeper to listen to Audrey, but nothing worked. Nora had made up her mind.

"Don't worry, I'll come out and see the place – and I'll bring cookies!" she smiled. "It's much more comfortable for me here and someone should keep an eye on the house. I think my sister from Chicago might come for a visit and Mr. Zimmermann will keep me company, too." At the mention of Mr. Zimmermann, the teens exchanged subtle smiles. They had watched the courtship between the housekeeper and her new boyfriend and they were happy for her.

"Besides, I think you might appreciate me more by the end of the summer if you have to cook and clean up after yourselves for a while," Nora smiled when she said that, but there was a serious tone to her voice. As much as she loved the three teenagers in her kitchen, she also believed in discipline, and in her own way she was strict with them.

"Before you young people leave, we have a birthday party to plan!" Nora exclaimed. Audrey's birthday was so soon after the end of the school year, Nora always said it was literally the icing on the cake. The plan was to celebrate the 15th birthday at home and leave for Lake Bonita the next day.

"Are we still on for chocolate cake?" Nora looked like a fairy tale grandmother when she asked the question.

"Of course, with chocolate frosting!" came Audrey's prompt reply. It sounded like the woman and the girl had been rehearsing their lines for years.

"What did you guys get me?" Audrey always asked about presents, even though she knew she wouldn't get any answers, and she always got some laughs. The girl looked even prettier when her big brown eyes opened wide and a smile lit up her face.

Mr. Conroy's arrival interrupted Audrey's little joke. He walked into the kitchen with his cell phone plastered to his ear, obviously in the middle of a serious conversation. He smiled distractedly at his daughter and the others as he set his briefcase down on the kitchen counter, awkwardly trying to shake off his coat with one hand while still holding the phone to his ear. Audrey jumped up to help her father with his coat and then waited silently until he finished his conversation.

"So school is finally over - congratulations!" said the man with forced joviality, greeting Audrey with a quick kiss on her forehead. "I think I remember what a great feeling that was..." He looked distracted.

"Is everything OK, Dad?" Audrey asked tentatively. She rarely saw her father look as stressed as he did at the moment.

"The stock market crashed today. My clients are panicking and my phone is ringing off the hook. It looks pretty bad." He managed to smile warmly at his daughter, "Sorry sweetheart, you don't want to hear business stuff on a day like today." He looked around the group. "What are you guys doing to celebrate the great escape from school for one more summer? Pizza? A movie? My treat. Who knows – it might be the last one for a while," he added grimly. "Don't worry Audrey, we already bought your birthday present!" With that he burst out laughing, much to the relief of everybody else in the kitchen.

Mr. Conroy needed his sense of humor to get through the next few days. The stock market crash had a huge impact on his business, forcing him to reconsider the family plans for the summer at the lake house. He had been a stock broker for years and had never seen anything like it. Mrs. Conroy's real estate business was in turmoil as well, so after much deliberation both of Audrey's parents decided it would be best for them to stay at home for the summer. The news was a huge disappointment to the teenagers, even though they understood the reasons behind it.

Audrey's parents suggested that Nora go as a chaperone in their place and the three teens started a relentless campaign to convince the housekeeper to accompany them, but to no avail. Not even Dakota's high school German worked on "Frau Nora." No amount of pleading was going to make her assume sole responsibility for three teenagers for an entire summer. The enthusiasm the teens had felt about the summer ahead of them was dampened, but they tried to stay positive. After all, it was still summer.

It was the very busy and very business-like Mrs. Conroy who came up with a solution - why couldn't Erin and Dakota's father chaperone at the lake house? If the kids made good on their promise to help with the housework and the cooking, Mr. Harris would be able to write. Sadie could go, too, and keep Patches company. This time, Mrs. Conroy decided to discuss the idea with the adults before presenting it to the teens.

Mr. Conroy loved the idea, but Mr. Harris was less than thrilled. He had been uncomfortable with the idea of accepting such a generous invitation from the start, even for his children, and if he were to go, too, it would mean accepting even more of the Conroy's generosity. However, in the minds of Mr. and Mrs. Conroy, their neighbor would be doing them a favor. In the end, Mr. Harris swallowed his pride and agreed to go for the sake of their children. Alan and Alecia Conroy promised to drive out to the lake as often as they could.

"Thank you, thank you, thank you, Mr. Harris!" Audrey's gratitude was sincere, but she was clearly over the top with her expression of it. She kept saying over and over that the summer at the lake was her best present ever in all her 15 years, thanks to Mr. Harris. The two families were gathered at the Conroy's to celebrate Audrey's birthday.

"If I were Mr. Harris, I would seriously be reconsidering my offer right about now," Mrs. Conroy cautioned her daughter. "Give the man some peace and quiet. As it is, he's going to have his hands full with the three of you starting tomorrow."

"Thanks, Alecia!" Mr. Harris smiled at Audrey's mother, obviously relieved when she got her daughter to stop thanking him. "Wait until she sees what a slave-driver I am. She'll change her tune soon enough." It was funny how Mr. Harris could make jokes about himself. He really was strict with his children, but somehow they always, or almost always, understood that he was only trying to do the right thing for them. Audrey had experienced this first hand since she had become friends with Erin and Dakota, but so far she had never complained when Mr. Harris disciplined them. Her own parents were usually too busy to be very involved in her life and Audrey found something comforting in the close relationship Mr. Harris had with Erin and Dakota. She often wondered what Mrs.

Harris had been like, but she was reluctant to ask her friends questions about their mother because they were still so sad.

Audrey's thoughts were interrupted when Nora entered the room with a magnificent chocolate cake ablaze with 15 candles, prompting a horrendous version of Happy Birthday. There wasn't a good singer in the group, but there were certainly some loud and enthusiastic voices. Audrey loved the attention. The dogs ran around like crazy trying to join in the fun, or maybe their ears just hurt from the horrible singing. The birthday girl opened her presents with a dramatic flair, and Erin marveled at how much her friend loved the spotlight. The two girls were best friends, but they definitely had different personalities. Erin smiled to herself, glad that Audrey was her friend.

Chapter 4

Summer!

It took Audrey forever to get all her things together the morning after her birthday, even though she had been packing for the lake house since school ended. She kept running back into the house to get something else she just had to bring with her or one more birthday present – like the new camera her parents had given her. Mrs. Conroy was just as busy, determined to make sure her daughter had everything she could possibly need for the summer – and then some. While Audrey and her parents produced a mountain of bags, Patches ran back and forth from the house to the car non-stop, determined not to miss anything.

Mr. Harris concluded that Audrey was bringing more luggage than his entire family combined, a thought he politely kept to himself. When everything was finally squeezed into their already crowded SUV, everybody gathered in the driveway to say goodbye. Mr. and Mrs. Conroy would be coming out to the lake as often as they could, but it suddenly occurred to Nora that she might not see Audrey all summer, and it made her very emotional.

Once they were on the road, Mr. Harris realized just how excited the teenagers were and he was glad he had agreed to go.

"What do you have in all those suitcases, Audrey?" Dakota could not resist teasing their friend. "This is summer at a lake house, not a fashion show. Nora even called it a camp, remember?" Audrey just ignored him. She needed her clothes. She was always impeccably dressed and that would not change over the summer, camp or no camp.

"Or is all that for Patches?" Dakota tried to tease her one more time, laughing at his own joke, but Audrey continued to ignore him. When she turned and started talking to Erin about their plans for the summer, Dakota finally gave up and started a conversation with his father about history - their favorite topic. Dakota had scheduled an interview for a summer job on the landscaping crew at Monticello and he was nervous about it because the idea of working at Thomas Jefferson's home was probably the most exciting thing he could imagine. His father enjoyed the opportunity to give the boy some tips, especially since Dakota rarely asked for advice these days.

Girl talk and interview tips made the three hour drive pass quickly, but all conversation ended abruptly when the car pulled into the driveway of the rental house. Leaves were still knee-deep in the yard and on the deck and the windows were still filthy, contrary to the promises the realtor had made. Mr. Harris took his usual calm, conservative approach.

"Let's see what's been done inside before we get upset about anything," he said as they piled out of the car. He remembered Mrs. Conroy's complaints about the place, but as soon as he saw the surface of the lake shimmering through the trees he totally ignored the leaves. Still admiring the view as he climbed the steps to the wrap-around deck, Mr. Harris was pleased to see that major repairs had recently been made to the rickety looking deck. The boards that had been replaced were a bright, fresh color which stood out next to the original decking, and all of the support beams and braces looked like they were new. The deck had been one point even Mr. Conroy had stressed. *At least the place looks safe, if not particularly clean*, thought Mr. Harris. A fleeting image of Alecia Conroy freaking out about the leaves flashed through his mind as he turned to follow the kids and the dogs into the house. He felt more than just a pang of guilt when he realized how grateful he was that Mrs. Conroy wasn't with them.

Mr. Harris fell in love with the rambling structure as quickly as his children had, especially when he saw the master bedroom on the main floor which was going to be his domain. It was a huge room with a massive desk positioned in an alcove overlooking the lake. It was perfect for writing, but more importantly, he would be able to keep an eye on what was happening around the house and on the water.

The girls immediately started dragging their (Audrey's) bags to the upstairs bedrooms, eager to stake their claim as soon as possible. Dakota showed his father the rest of the house, including the downstairs area which was Dakota's by default. It was a little dark and a little damp and not particularly clean, but the boy loved it. There were two connecting bedrooms, a storage room, a small bathroom and a laundry room. One bedroom had a sliding glass door which opened out to the path leading down to the lake, but the brush was so thick you could barely even see the water. The whole downstairs felt like a cave. Perfect. Maybe Dakota would find some artifacts inside the house, too.

As they explored the rest of the house, it was hard to tell who was more excited – the teenagers or the dogs or Mr. Harris. There was an apologetic note in the kitchen from the realtor explaining that a cleaning team would be there tomorrow for the entire day. Next to the note she had left a phone book, a map of the area and a coupon for two free pizzas. Dinner…

None of them slept well that first night, in spite of being exhausted. The house had no central air conditioning and the loud window AC units kept everybody awake, but it was too warm to turn them off. The teens had devoured their pizza on the deck and stayed up late, talking excitedly about how they were going to spend their summer while they watched the moonlight reflected on the water and the lights of an occasional boat passing by. The warm summer breeze and the sounds from the lake and the trees held the promise of something wonderful.

Breakfast the next morning was pretty much the same as dinner and it appeared the groundwork for their summer routine had been established. After a late start, they lingered a long time on the deck again, just enjoying the view. Most of the afternoon was spent organizing stuff and driving around, shopping for groceries and other supplies while a cleaning crew tackled the layers of grime in the house. It had been productive, but not fun. Mr. Harris thought kayaking would be just the thing to end the afternoon with some excitement, so he called the realtor to ask if she could recommend a local instructor. It all came together quickly and he was able to surprise the kids with a private kayak lesson late that afternoon.

"Use your core - don't just use your arms to paddle!" Jamie, the kayak instructor, patiently repeated everything at least twice to get all four of his students to understand him. He had brought two of his own kayaks with all the gear so that Erin, Audrey, Dakota and Mr. Harris could have a lesson together.

Jamie's passion for kayaking was obvious. He gave his students a brief tutorial on dry land and showed them the proper way to cinch up their life jackets before allowing anybody to get in the water. He stayed calm amid the flying paddles and endless questions that came from the group as they practiced on dry land. Once they were actually on the water in the brightly colored kayaks, he gave each of them enough attention so that they were all able to maneuver a boat on their own, at least somewhat, by the end of the lesson. Of course, Dakota was a natural. The others did okay.

Jamie made them promise to always wear a life jacket on the water and never kayak alone, and he told them they were welcome to call him anytime they needed help. After the instructor left, the already soaked teens went for a swim while Mr. Harris made hamburgers for dinner. They had all agreed to rotate the dinner shift and Mr. Harris had volunteered to go first. Erin liked the idea of sharing the cooking, but she was more than a little apprehensive about eating anything her brother cooked. In the end, she decided to try it because they all agreed it would be fair – and definitely interesting.

It had been a great day. They gravitated to the deck again for dinner and spent the evening outside playing dice, listening to the tree frogs and cicadas, and giving Dakota encouragement for his job interview in the morning. He was excited about it and of course he couldn't stop talking about Thomas Jefferson and Monticello. Erin and Audrey grinned at each other as they listened to the conversation between Dakota and Mr. Harris, but they didn't say much. The girls were content just to watch the lights come on in the houses across the lake as the sun set over the water. They stayed up late again. It was a great start to the summer.

A rather sleepy Dakota took the car to Monticello the next morning after promising his father to be extra careful on the winding roads. The girls opted for a short walk with the dogs before venturing out in the kayaks. Of course, they also had to promise Mr. Harris to be careful on the water and to stay where he could see them from his desk. He could see a lot of the lake from his perch and he assured the girls he would be watching. The beautiful setting at the lake house motivated him to write and he was eager to get to work on his book.

Erin and Audrey were giggling like crazy by the time they actually climbed into the kayaks, probably from being so tired. As they paddled away from the dock into the main part of the lake, they were startled by a small fishing boat almost hidden under the tree limbs, just below the house. The two men in the boat were just as startled and they quickly dropped whatever it was they were hauling up out of the water back into the lake. It struck both girls as rather odd behavior. Audrey said good morning to the men, but they barely even acknowledged her greeting, so the girls exchanged knowing looks and headed out into the lake without saying another word.

One kayaking lesson was barely enough to get the two novices across the lake, but they did their best and they had fun. Lacking technical skills meant more work for them with every paddle stroke - they experienced some wild swaying and near capsizes, but the water was so inviting neither one of them was too worried about an accidental swim. Besides, there was very little boat traffic on the lake and they managed to reach the public beach on the far shore without incident.

"Look, Erin!" Audrey said, pointing to a mansion on the shore. "We saw the lights from that house while we were out on our deck last night. It looks even bigger from here. Boy, it's gorgeous!" Audrey was used to nice things.

"I think your house is prettier," Erin commented while they dragged their boats up on the sandy beach.

"But our house isn't on a lake! I wonder what it's like to live here year round. I wonder how the schools are... Do you think the kids are nice?" Audrey had a habit of going off on tangents, much like Dakota.

"Did we bring any granola bars?" Erin changed the subject, but part of her mind was already thinking about what it would be like to live here – even though it was impossible for her to imagine leaving Dunellon.

The girls chatted aimlessly while they ate their snacks, easily falling into the lazy mindset of a hot summer day. The lake was perfect – clear and quiet and right at their feet. They cooled off with a short swim before putting the boats back in the water. After they started paddling away from the beach, Audrey glanced back at the house she admired so much and quickly signaled to Erin with her paddle. Walking down the impressive lawn to the water were two boys, about Dakota's age, surrounded by a pack of beautiful brown and white dogs. Audrey had to look twice – she thought she was seeing things because the two boys were identical. By the time Erin turned to see what was so interesting, the boys were already waving to

Audrey and gesturing to her to paddle over. It never took boys long to notice Audrey.

The girls looked at each other with the same questioning expression on their faces. "Let's paddle over there and say hello," Audrey said tentatively, knowing she would have to talk her friend into it. "We don't even have to get out of the boats. It would be nice to meet some kids from around here."

Erin thought of her father watching from across the lake. "Okay, but seriously, let's not get out of the boats."

As they paddled back towards the shore, the girls noticed the immaculate grounds surrounding the big house. Everything looked better the closer they got - the house, the landscaping, the boys – even the dogs. Erin stayed a little ways behind Audrey while the boys walked down to the water and introduced themselves.

"I'm Daniel and this is David," said the first boy, pointing behind him. "Yes, we're twins," he added nonchalantly, as if he had said it a thousand times (which he probably had.) The two boys, or rather, young men, were incredibly good looking and exuded self-confidence, even from a distance. They both had jet-black hair and dark eyes and perfect white teeth. Erin was a little intimidated, but Audrey started talking immediately. She told the boys about the house they were renting for the summer and pointed it out across the lake behind the trees. Then she asked them if they went to school at the lake and what there was to do for fun, besides the water. Daniel told the girls about their private school in DC which really got Audrey's attention – she had just moved from there last year.

Audrey chatted while Erin sat quietly and watched the dogs on the expansive lawn. They were beautiful animals and there were a lot of them. David, the quiet twin, saw Erin admiring the dogs and spoke directly to her.

"They're American Staffordshire Terriers," he explained. "My Dad breeds them. He shows them, too."

Erin smiled at the boy, "They really are beautiful," she told him, still admiring the dogs. All of them had a white stripe down their nose, except for one loner who had a jagged white marking on his forehead. "That one looks like Harry Potter with his lightning bolt scar. I like him!" Erin was starting to warm up a little when a middle-aged man in riding boots appeared from around the corner with an armful of leashes.

The man acknowledged the girls in their kayaks and the boys on the lawn with a hasty, but polite, nod before he turned his attention to the dogs. With a short whistle and one simple hand signal, every single dog turned to face the man and sat down at attention. Erin was fascinated. She had never seen anything like it.

Audrey decided it was time to leave. "Come on Erin, let's get going," she prompted and then looked back to say goodbye to the boys. "We'll see you guys around," she said, waving as she paddled away, but then she turned around again and asked the boys if they had kayaks.

"We do, but we really like big boats," said Daniel with a confident smile. "We have a party boat and a speed boat for water skiing – you should come with us sometime." He waved goodbye to the girls and started back to the house with his brother.

"Pretty dogs," said Erin as they paddled away. "Did you see the one with the lightning bolt on his forehead?"

"What a gorgeous house!" Audrey started talking as if she hadn't listened to a word Erin said. "Everything about it was gorgeous! Even the dogs! Do you think Patches and Sadie would get along with those dogs? I'm sure they'd love living in a house like that. I know I would."

Erin concentrated on her kayaking while her friend rambled on about the fancy house and the boys during their paddle back home. Once they reached their side of the lake, Erin noticed the little fishing boat with the two strange men was gone, but something floating on the surface of the lake caught her eye. She paddled over and saw that it was just a leaf reflecting the brilliant midday sun. She sat under the trees for a moment watching the pattern on the water made by the shade of the over-hanging limbs and just enjoyed the beautiful view. It was so peaceful.

Erin was jolted back to reality by the sound of her brother's voice echoing across the water.

"I got the job! I start Monday! I am going to work for Thomas Jefferson!" Dakota was shouting and waving at them with a huge grin on his face. Erin and Audrey smiled broadly at each other and quickly made their way to the dock. Dakota's enthusiasm was contagious. He helped the girls get their boats out of the water, talking the whole time about his new job at Monticello.

They were all soaked by the time they were finished, a perfect excuse to jump in the lake. Mr. Harris called down from the deck and let the dogs out to join them. Patches and Sadie both loved the water, but in very different ways and it was really cool to be able to go swimming with them. Patches would fly down to the edge of the lake and put all four brakes on as soon as she was ankle deep in the water, then promptly lie down. She never actually went swimming, but she wiggled around in shallow water, thoroughly enjoying herself and wagging her tail the entire time.

Sadie was a different story. Swimming came naturally to her and she would swim after sticks or a ball until she was exhausted. Dakota spent the afternoon trying to teach her to jump off the dock, which was absolutely hilarious because the big happy dog just wouldn't do it. Peals of laughter and dog barks echoed across the water and the would-be dog trainer got waves and smiles from everybody riding by in boats when they saw what he was trying to do. It was a blast and they were all exhausted by the time Mr. Harris showed up on the dock. Erin tried to get her father to join them for a swim, but she couldn't talk him into it.

"I can enjoy the water very well from right here, thank you! It's not quite hot enough for me to brave the water yet. But I did get in that kayak yesterday, remember?" he asked proudly. "Are you guys getting hungry? I thought we could go out for dinner tonight to celebrate Dakota's good news. Nothing fancy, just one of the local restaurants." He paused, "Besides, I have to admit I'm a little leery of eating Dakota's cooking. What gourmet delight were you planning to cook for us tonight, Cody?"

Everybody laughed, including Dakota. "I kind of forgot about it Dad...sorry."

"I think we should let Cody off the hook for the entire summer, at least as far as cooking is concerned," Audrey suggested. "He's the only one of us who has a job, even if it is only part time. I don't mind helping out a little more, and it might be better for everybody - seriously," she added, smiling at Cody.

"Fine with me, but I bet Sadie will be disappointed," quipped Erin. "She was counting on mega leftovers!"

"Ha ha ha," Dakota countered, cannonballing off the dock with a loud "Yeehaw!"

Chapter 5

The Nature Preserve

Erin woke up the next morning with a terrible earache. Her father advised her to stay out of the water for a couple of days and she reluctantly agreed, but she was disappointed. Audrey was disappointed, too, because the girls had been looking forward to another paddle. Erin suggested that Dakota take Audrey kayaking, but he wanted to treat the girls to miniature golf in celebration of his new job. In the end they agreed on both – a morning paddle and afternoon mini-golf.

After another leisurely breakfast and a group dog walk, Erin decided to explore the nature preserve next to the house while Audrey and Dakota kayaked.   The heavily wooded preserve had been tempting her ever since she had first seen it and a walk through the woods was the next best thing to being on the lake in a kayak. She was actually looking forward to walking alone, but it made her father nervous, so she promised him she would carry her cell phone and take Sadie with her, too.

From the beginning of the trail, Erin could see her brother and Audrey putting the boats in the water, but she quickly lost sight of them as she entered the nature preserve. It was incredibly peaceful in the woods even though the birds made a huge racket. Sadie had her nose to the ground from the get-go, loving every minute of it. They followed a narrow path through the trees, each enjoying the walk in their own way. Erin was totally lost in her thoughts when she rounded a bend and was suddenly jolted out of her reverie. What she saw made her freeze in her tracks and she almost had to pinch herself to make sure she wasn't dreaming.

Huge rhododendrons lined the trail on either side, making it quite narrow in the curve of the path. As Erin looked through the thick branches to see what lay behind them, she spotted a flash of white in the dark woods. About fifty feet away from her stood a beautiful, young, totally white deer. It was magic, like something out of a fairy tale. If it had been brown, Erin never would have seen it in the dense foliage, but the animal's bright white color stood out like a light in the dark. The fawn's head was raised and its two big pink ears were at attention, looking just as surprised as the girl. For a fleeting moment, the two creatures stood looking right into each other's eyes. All Erin could think of was a unicorn.

The magic was broken as soon as Sadie discovered the deer and bolted towards it, jerking Erin back to reality at the other end of the leash and sending the shy creature flying off into the woods. Erin stood silently for a moment, wondering if what she had just seen was real or a figment of her imagination. *Did she have a fever from her ear infection?* When she started walking again, a feeling of amazement grew within her as she realized how special it was to have come face to face with an albino, pink ears and all! The image of the graceful white fawn staring at her was lodged in her brain and she found it difficult to think of anything else. She started following the path aimlessly and let Sadie dictate the pace for the rest of the walk, which meant stopping almost every foot to let the dog investigate all the exciting forest smells along the way. Erin didn't mind at all.

The trail wasn't as long as Erin thought it would be and she soon found herself on the far side of the preserve, on one of the little side streets of the lake community. The houses here were small and there was something cozy about the tidy cottages and their neat little gardens. Absentmindedly, Erin decided to check out the neighborhood a little before she headed back home through the preserve. She was still lost in her thoughts about the beautiful white deer and she let Sadie lead her along the quiet street like a guide dog.

Erin jumped straight up in the air and almost fell over when a voice out of nowhere brought her back to reality. She looked around and realized she had been standing in front of a wildly overgrown garden while Sadie went to town sniffing. The voice she heard belonged to a rather scruffy looking boy standing behind a fence in a patch of sunflowers, smiling shyly at her. His blond hair was long and unkempt, much like the yard he was standing in, and a ton of even scruffier looking dogs were gathering around him to greet Sadie through the fence. The overgrown yard looked out of place next to the other neat gardens on the little street.

In spite of the totally disheveled appearance of everything she saw, Erin sensed something friendly and nice about the boy and all his dogs.

"Hi," she said. "I'm sorry. I guess I wasn't paying attention. I was kind of lost in my thoughts."

"Did you see the albino in the nature preserve?" asked the boy matter-of-factly. His smile broadened as he watched the expression on Erin's face change to amazement.

"How did you know?" she asked. "You've seen it, too? So I didn't imagine it!" There was relief in her voice.

"Yep, it's real," the boy reassured her. "A lot of people won't believe you if you talk about it, but I don't care - I'm just glad every time I see it. You kind of had that look on your face when I saw you. It's awesome." The boy paused and then walked around through a gate so he could give Sadie a scratch behind the ears and introduce himself. "I'm Tommy, and these are all our rescue dogs. My Mom goes a little overboard with the dogs, but I don't mind. They're all nice and I hate to think of them in the pound...or worse."

Erin smiled back and introduced herself. She found herself warming up to the friendly boy, which was quite unlike her usual reserved nature around people she didn't know. She told Tommy about the house they were renting and about her brother and her father and Audrey and Sadie and Patches. When she found herself telling a total stranger about her ear infection, she stopped abruptly and burst out laughing.

"That albino must have really gone to my head!" she said, still laughing. "I don't usually go on like that."

"It's OK," said Tommy sincerely. "I understand. I see it almost every morning and – oh sorry – that's my mother - I have to go. See you 'round!" A beat up old car had just pulled into the driveway and a spry little woman got out and waved at them as she carried grocery bags into the house. The boy waved goodbye to Erin and turned to go back to the little house with peeling paint and wildly overgrown yard.

"Bye, Tommy!" Erin called after him and she was pleased when he turned around and gave her another wave and a big smile.

Two unusual encounters in one morning, thought Erin as she made her way back to the preserve. She gave Sadie a treat from her pocket and they set out at a good pace as they turned back down the little street to head home.

Audrey and Dakota were swimming when Erin got back to the house. Mr. Harris was on the deck, calling everybody in for lunch, and he motioned for Erin to join him. She pulled the makings for sandwiches out of the fridge without paying much attention to what she was doing and set paper plates and paper towels on the table on the deck. They really weren't fancy.

"Yoo-hoo, Erin - anybody there?" asked her father good-naturedly. "I've been talking to you for five minutes and I don't think you heard a single word I said."

"Sorry, Dad, I guess I was daydreaming," answered Erin sheepishly. She realized she was reluctant to share her albino story with her father for some reason, but she didn't know why.

He asked how her ear felt, but before Erin could answer Audrey burst into the kitchen with Dakota. "Those men in the boat were out there again," she said excitedly. "One of them was diving." Her face looked serious.

"Yeah, but they wouldn't tell us what they were looking for," Dakota added. "I think they're up to something, Dad!" The boy had a vivid imagination.

"Let's see, son," said Mr. Harris slowly. "We're on a lake. It's summer. Those men have a boat. Yep, sounds suspicious to me." He laughed and patted Dakota affectionately on the back. "It's a good thing you start working next week. Otherwise I'd really have to keep an eye on you around here. By the way, we have to talk about getting you to and from work. I don't really like the idea of being stuck here without a car, even if it is just four hours a day. I'll let you take the car on Monday if you promise to ask around for a ride after that. I'm sure there must be some people who work at Monticello and live around here."

"Sure, Dad. We should have brought Old Blue," said Dakota, referring to their mother's old car. Mr. Harris had given it to Dakota last Christmas and the boy had quickly gotten used to having a car of his own. The girls also enjoyed having a willing chauffeur.

"I know," his father agreed. "Maybe we can get it when I go back home to meet my agent." Then he quickly added, "But you're not driving back up here by yourself."

Dakota knew better than to argue with his father about things like that, so he just followed the others out to the deck for lunch without saying a word.

"How was your walk this morning?" Audrey asked Erin in front of a miniature lighthouse at the miniature golf course. Dakota had made good on his promise to treat the girls to putt-putt after lunch.

Erin hesitated so long before answering that both Dakota and Audrey were looking at her curiously by the time she finally spoke.

"It was great," Erin said slowly. "I saw an albino deer in the woods and I met a nice guy with a ton of dogs who lives on the other side of the preserve." For some reason, it was a relief to finally talk about her little adventure. The other two teens made her tell all the details and as she talked, Erin realized how significant both encounters had been for her, but she still wasn't sure why.

"All I could think of was a unicorn when I saw that deer. It was beautiful, like something out of a fairy tale. It even had pink eyes! Tommy said he's seen it, too, but nobody believes him."

"I'd like to meet this Tommy," said Dakota in a protective manner.

"I think you'd like him," said Erin. "He's a lot nicer than those twins we met yesterday."

"What twins?" asked Dakota, his tone even more protective than before.

"They're fine, Erin," Audrey insisted. To Dakota, she explained, "They live in that gorgeous house across the lake. Even their dogs are gorgeous. We met them when we took the kayaks out yesterday."

"I don't know," said Erin. "I think they were a little stuck up, actually maybe a lot stuck up."

"That's just because their parents have money. I knew a slew of kids like that when we lived in DC," Audrey said, brushing it off. "Boy would I love to see the inside of that house. Maybe my mother can get us inside when she comes to visit."

Erin and Dakota had to laugh at Audrey's love of the finer things in life. Both brother and sister thought the world of their friend, but she certainly was materialistic at times. The Conroy family and the Harris family were at opposite ends of the money spectrum.

"What's so funny?" Audrey asked defensively, but she already knew the answer. "Oh, never mind," she said, picking up her putter. When she hit the ball right into one of the revolving blades of a windmill, they all cracked up.

"Well tomorrow I'd like to meet your new friends – all of them," Dakota stated seriously. "Let's go for a walk in the preserve in the morning to look for Erin's magical creature and her new two-legged friend. Audrey, you and I can kayak across the lake tomorrow afternoon to meet those twins." He was being the authoritative big brother again. "This could be a long summer if you girls keep meeting boys. How big are they?" he asked, laughing.

"When do you start work?" muttered Erin under her breath, but Dakota was already focused on showing Audrey the right way to play the windmill shot and didn't hear his sister's remark.

Chapter 6

Monticello

Dakota was serious about meeting the girls' new "friends" and he insisted on following through right after breakfast the next day. Of course, once all three teens were in the woods they made enough noise to scare away a herd of elephants, so there was no way they were going to see any deer, especially the shy albino. It didn't help matters any to have two enthusiastic dogs on the trail with them, but the early morning walk was good for Sadie and Patches because it was so much cooler then. Erin felt the sense of wonder return when she showed the others the rhododendron patch where she had seen the albino. Audrey and Dakota didn't seem all that impressed.

"Let's go meet that boy," Audrey directed, moving on down the path with Patches. "I want to see what he looks like."

It turned out they were 0 for 2. Tommy's yard was empty – except for the dogs, of course, who greeted them eagerly through the fence. Erin could tell that Audrey was about to comment on the total mess of the yard and the house, but Erin silenced her friend with one direct look. Audrey returned the look with one of those smiles that spoke volumes. The two girls understood each other very well and had a healthy respect for each other's differences.

"This is boring," declared Dakota. "Let's go back and get the kayaks. Erin, how long are you going to stay out of the water?"

"I don't know, probably another day or two. I don't want this earache to get so bad I have to go to the doctor or stay out of the water all summer." Erin was so practical. "You guys go kayaking and I'll get Dad to take me grocery shopping. It's my turn to make dinner tonight. I thought I'd make a big salad."

"Wunderbar." Dakota used his favorite German word. Steak and salad sounds great." The boy liked his food.

"I said salad," Erin corrected. "I was thinking with garlic bread, but I guess I can find some meat for you. Dad would probably like that, too."

The dogs decided it was time to move on, so the teens let their four-legged friends lead the way home. If the albino was anywhere nearby, she was smart enough to hide from the boisterous group.

Erin was a good cook. She had started making dinner for her family on weekends after her mother died and she enjoyed it. Nora, the Conroy's housekeeper, was always encouraging her with cooking tips and recipes so Erin was slowly starting to feel more self-confident in the kitchen.

"Good job, Erin!" her father praised during dinner on the deck.

"Great job!" echoed Audrey.

"Mmmm. Funny looking steak," mused Dakota, holding up a piece of grilled chicken on his fork.

"I'm just glad you're not cooking this summer," Audrey quipped, looking directly at Dakota. "Who knows what we'd end up eating."

Erin changed the subject before her brother could answer with some corny remark. "Did you guys see the twins this afternoon?"

"As a matter of fact, we did," answered Audrey. "And guess what? We're all invited to a party at their house on the Fourth of July! I can't wait to see the inside of that place."

"What was your impression, Cody? Didn't you think they were a little snooty?" This question came from Erin.

"They're OK. I kind of understand what you're talking about, but they're not that bad. I think they're just two guys trying to be cool." Dakota didn't seem to care one way or the other about the twins. "Nice dogs, though," he added with a little more enthusiasm.

"We paddled down to the shallow end of the lake today and it was totally different there away from all the motor boats. I can't really explain it." Dakota paused, obviously thinking about how to describe what he meant.

"The houses looked kind of dark and spooky, like they were abandoned – but they weren't," Audrey helped him out. "And they looked really old. I got some pretty interesting pictures." Audrey hadn't gone anywhere without her camera since they arrived at the lake. It was waterproof.

"I thought we had an agreement about where you could go in the kayaks," interjected Mr. Harris in a serious tone.

"I know Dad, but we stayed together and we paddled close to shore the whole way," Dakota explained in their defense.

"And we wore our life jackets and we had my cell phone in a dry bag," Audrey added, trying to help her friend with their defense.

"Besides," Dakota continued, "you weren't even here – you were out grocery shopping with Erin."

"OK, OK'" Mr. Harris conceded. "Just be careful."

"We will," Dakota promised.

"I don't think we'll be going back there anyway," said Audrey. "It was like something out of *Lord of the Rings* – you know, the middle book that's so dark and depressing."

"*The Two Towers*," offered Erin.

"It was definitely weird." Dakota paused for a moment before switching gears completely. "Hey, can I interest you guys in a tour of Monticello before I start working there? I think they have something going on this weekend - like an open house or start of summer or something like that. I'm sure it'll be awesome."

Mr. Harris loved the idea, but the girls looked skeptical. Erin exchanged a knowing look with Audrey before turning to her father.

"We'll go as long as we can set a time limit," said Erin firmly. "Whenever you and Cody get into a place like that you forget about everything else and want to stay forever. It's like being stuck in 'The Twilight Zone' or some kind of time warp."

"I can see the news story now," said Audrey dramatically, *"Family Trapped in Monticello."* Erin was the only one who laughed.

"It wouldn't hurt for you girls to visit Monticello," Mr. Harris said. "Who knows? You might even enjoy it. Let's go Saturday afternoon and we'll go out for pizza afterwards. What do you say?"

Pizza was the one food all three teenagers agreed on and Mr. Harris knew how to use it to his advantage.

Thomas Jefferson's beautiful Monticello sat on top of a hill in the rolling Virginia countryside. It was a brick house with majestic white pillars and a white round cupola, but it was much smaller than the girls had expected. Dakota and his father were unconditionally thrilled from the start, but even the reluctant girls found a lot to like. The grounds were gorgeous and there was a lot going on. Between the tours of the main house, the outbuildings, the gardens, and all of the demonstrations, it was easy to picture what life must have been like on the plantation 200 years ago.

Dakota was thrilled. He hung on every word the tour guides said, both inside the house and out, and he told anybody who would listen to him that he was starting work at Monticello on Monday. He and his father loved all of Jefferson's inventions and gadgets, but they were especially impressed with the copy machine Jefferson had rigged up. Mr. Harris said it was a great example of creativity and resourcefulness. The writer would insert his hand into a metal sleeve and grip a pen. As he wrote, a second pen attached to bars on the metal sleeve followed the movement of the first pen, making an exact copy of all the strokes. Jefferson wrote a lot of letters and he kept copies of everything he sent, so this invention had saved him a tremendous amount of time.

"Contrary to popular belief, Thomas Jefferson did not invent this copy machine," explained the guide. "But he probably used it more than anyone else. He was a brilliant correspondent."

Erin and Audrey must have exchanged about a million "Oh, Brother!" looks during the tour, but it was all good-natured. They knew Dakota would be reciting endless stories about Thomas Jefferson over the summer, even if he was only going to be mowing the historical presidential lawn. Both girls were impressed with Monticello and enjoyed their visit, but each for very different reasons. Erin loved the beautifully landscaped grounds with their incredible variety of flowers and vegetables, and Audrey loved the antiques in the main house and spent a small fortune in the gift shop. What a surprise!

The rest of the weekend flew by. It rained all day Sunday, so the kids rented movies and played games and Erin and Audrey made spaghetti and meatballs for dinner. The rain came straight down in such a steady stream they were able to keep the windows open all day without soaking the inside of the house. It was a cozy feeling, almost like a blanket over the house. The dogs seemed ready for a lazy day indoors, too, especially after a week of walks and swimming. Mr. Harris spent most of the rainy day writing in his room, emerging only sporadically for coffee. Each time he filled his cup, he paused for a moment to stare out the window, saying how much he loved the sound of the rain. Everybody agreed with him.

The Conroys called late in the day to let everybody know they would be coming to the lake house the following weekend. Audrey seemed pleased, but the minute she hung up she said they had a lot of cleaning to do before her mother got there. Nobody contradicted her. The cleaning team sent by the realtor had managed to improve things somewhat, but everybody knew the house would not meet Mrs. Conroy's approval.

Mr. Harris suggested that he and Dakota drive back to Dunellon to get Old Blue over the weekend while the Conroys were visiting. He felt a twinge of guilt when he silently rejoiced about missing Mrs. Conroy's visit, but everybody agreed it would be great to have two cars at the lake, especially since Dakota would be working. It was a plan.

As expected, Dakota fell in love with his new job. He was half an hour early on his first day of work and he came home with a huge grin on his face. Actually, he grinned all day. He just loved it. He told his father he found someone he could carpool with for the rest of the week and he described every minute of his first day in detail. Nobody was surprised at his enthusiasm – they were all happy for him and even the girls listened patiently while he told his stories. Dakota pretty much talked through the entire afternoon and only slowed down a little bit during the taco dinner Audrey made for them. He couldn't wait to go back in the morning.

The summer routine at the lake house was shaping up nicely. Erin's earache was better, but she decided to stay out of the water for a few more days. She told her father she wanted to play it safe, but the real reason was that she wanted to look for the albino. She started walking in the nature preserve every morning - sometimes before the others were even up - and every day she fell more in love with the woods and the wildlife. Audrey didn't seem too interested in the early morning walks, which was actually OK with Erin. She had the rest of the day to spend with her best friend, and besides, she quickly discovered that being alone for a little while in the morning was a great way to start the day. It made her feel good. Some mornings there was a heavy fog around the lake and it was like magic to watch the first rays of sunlight find their way through the thick branches of the trees and slowly burn away the morning mist. Erin found it peaceful and other-worldly.

By the end of the week, when she had all but given up hope of seeing the albino, Erin spotted the fawn in a clearing some distance from the path. The girl immediately froze and stood rooted to the spot, watching the graceful creature pick through the vegetation on the forest floor. Seeing the albino made Erin feel like she was in a fairy tale.

"Lucy," said Erin softly, wondering why on earth that name popped into her head. As if on cue, the white deer picked up its head and looked straight at the girl for what seemed like forever before bolting off into the cover of the woods. Erin stood silently for a long moment and a huge smile slowly spread across her face. She felt wonderful. She turned and made her way back home in a daze, oblivious to the raucous chorus of the early morning birds. "Lucy," she said softly to herself again, still smiling.

Of course, once Audrey saw the amazement on her friend's face she decided she had to see the albino, too. Erin hesitated, feeling guilty for not wanting to share this experience with her friend. She had no idea why she felt this way about the albino.

Audrey looked at her quizzically, picking up on her friend's hesitation, and made a tentative suggestion. "Maybe we could go for a walk together in the woods with Dakota when he gets home from work?"

"Sure," Erin quickly recovered, "but I don't know if we'll see her. I've been looking for her all week and this is the first time I saw her."

"Her?" Audrey asked. "How do you know it's a her? Does she have a name?"

Erin hesitated again before answering her best friend. "I named her Lucy. I don't know where the name came from – it just popped into my head." She was suddenly glad to be sharing all this with her friend.

"I like it," Audrey said, smiling. "It sounds like you. I would love to get a picture of her."

Chapter 7

Skateboarders

Mr. Conroy offered to drive Old Blue to the lake house when he and his wife came to visit, an offer which was promptly accepted. It was easy to talk Mrs. Conroy into driving their BMW - she loved that car and rarely got to drive it.

Even though none of them were keen on cleaning, everybody at the lake wanted to avoid upsetting Mrs. Conroy. Audrey's mother was a successful real estate broker and she liked everything around her to be as neat and organized as her business and her home. Unfortunately, that wasn't the case with the lake house, but the little group did their best to make it presentable. Erin had the brilliant idea to buy fresh flowers for the Conroy's room and put out gourmet cheese and crackers for their arrival.

Mr. Harris moved into the dungeon downstairs with Dakota on Friday so their "guests" could have the bedroom on the main floor - after all, the Conroys were paying for the house. The laundry and cleaning were finished well before the visitors were scheduled to arrive, and everybody agreed the house was presentable. That meant they all had the rest of the afternoon free. Audrey wanted to look for the albino again and she had no problem convincing Erin and Dakota to join her.

The shade of the trees offered a nice respite from the afternoon sun and it was especially welcome after a tedious burst of housework. Dakota rambled on about Monticello as usual, and as usual, Audrey and Erin listened without really paying much attention to him. They were both on the lookout for the little white deer, but each girl had her own idea of how to find the evasive creature. Audrey kept trying to analyze (out loud) what she would do if she were a shy deer in the woods and Erin kept trying to make the others stop talking so they wouldn't scare it away. Needless to say, they reached the other side of the preserve without seeing the albino or any other wild animals. Even the birds seemed much quieter than when Erin was alone.

"Let's go a little further and see if that boy Tommy is there. We still have plenty of time before my parents get here," Audrey suggested when they reached the far side of the woods. She was more curious about people than she was about animals anyway. No one objected, so the threesome left the shade of the woods for the blazing hot pavement. It wasn't long before they heard shouts and cheers coming from the general direction of Tommy's house. The noise was out of place in the quiet little neighborhood and it sparked the teens' curiosity.

As they rounded a corner onto one of the little side streets, Erin was almost run over by a gang of boys flying down the middle of the road on skateboards. There was a raw physical energy in the group which was a bit intimidating, especially for the girls. Erin and Audrey instinctively took a step closer to each other as Dakota moved forward and assumed a defensive stance in front of them.

"Watch where you're going!" a rough looking boy on a skateboard shouted to his friends. "You almost hit her!"

"Sorry," came a mumbled chorus of apologies as the boys stopped at the bottom of the street, flipped their boards up from their heels and caught them in mid-air.

Just as Dakota was revving up into hero mode, Erin spotted Tommy in the middle of the pack and waved to him. He waved back, a huge smile spreading across his face.

"Hi Erin!" he greeted her enthusiastically. "Hey guys, this is Erin," he continued with a sweep of his arm in her direction. "Erin, meet the guys." He looked just as scruffy as the first time Erin had seen him. As a matter of fact, the whole group was pretty rough looking.

"I'm Tommy," he said, walking towards the cautious newcomers. "You must be Erin's brother and you must be her friend." Tommy's friendly tone was a contrast to the rough and tumble behavior of the boys a few minutes earlier. Dakota relaxed his protective stance a little and gave Tommy a hesitant smile. Both girls were visibly relieved.

"You guys are crazy," Audrey stated bluntly, her brown eyes flashing. "You're going to kill yourselves on those things!" All five boys with skateboards burst out laughing and the tension in the air disappeared. They all started talking at once.

The two groups stood there in the middle of the road, talking for about half an hour. Dakota and Audrey let "the guys" convince them to try some very beginner skateboard stuff on level ground, but Erin wasn't the least bit tempted. She did come out of her shell a little bit, but mostly when she talked to Tommy. Erin felt comfortable around him, especially when he asked her about the albino.

"Have you seen it lately?" Tommy asked. "Mornings are the best time," he explained enthusiastically. "It's growing really fast. I think I need to give this fairy tale a name."

"Lucy," Erin said, surprising herself with her own openness. "I call her Lucy. Don't know where that came from..."

"Then Lucy it is!" Tommy announced. "I like giving animals names, especially the ones I like." He laughed under his breath. "All the mutts we have from the pound have names out of 'Harry Potter.'" Erin didn't respond, but his remark reminded her of the beautiful dog with the lightning bolt scar she had seen at the twins' house, the one she had named Harry. She was pleased to discover something she and Tommy had in common.

"Let's go girls," said Dakota authoritatively. Erin and Audrey rolled their eyes and looked at each other. It made them crazy when Dakota had one of his take-charge older brother moments.

"Yes sir!" said Audrey, saluting, and everybody laughed again. No matter where she was, Audrey quickly became popular. Erin said a quick goodbye to Tommy and waved to the others as she headed down the street to the woods with her brother and her friend. She didn't look back.

"What a ragged looking bunch of boys," Audrey commented to nobody in particular at the dinner table. "But they were nice," she quickly added, knowing her comment would be met with criticism from Erin.

"They're a lot nicer than the twins," came Erin's prompt reply, just as expected.

Of course this little exchange elicited a series of rapid-fire questions from Audrey's parents. The whole group was on the deck, squeezed around the little table covered with heaping platters of fried chicken, green beans, corn on the cob, salad and homemade biscuits. Apparently, Nora had been cooking for days because the Conroys had brought enough food to fill the refrigerator and the freezer with her homemade meals. The housekeeper was a wonderful cook and her gifts were a welcome change for the residents of the lake house, who enjoyed the respite from their own cooking. Audrey knew for a fact her mother was glad to have 'normal' food on the table because it made the 'camp' seem a little more like home for her.

Mrs. Conroy had started to complain the moment she opened her car door in the leaf-filled driveway, but her husband had somehow managed to prevent a tirade, encouraging her to just enjoy the time with her daughter and their friends. Mrs. Conroy listened to him, drawing on some of her maternal instincts which were usually buried deep beneath her very business-like exterior. The woman even seemed to be aware of the effect her presence had on Erin, which was very sensitive of her. Mrs. Conroy knew Erin missed her mother terribly, but neither of them was sure how to handle it. Mrs. Conroy was afraid she would make Erin feel worse by paying extra attention to her, and Erin was afraid of being too clingy to the no-nonsense Mrs. Conroy.

The flowers Erin had bought for the house gave Mrs. Conroy a perfect opportunity to give her a compliment and a big hug. Erin held on a bit too tightly for a bit too long, but that was OK. It wasn't often Mrs. Conroy showed much affection, even with her own daughter, and the woman was all business again as soon as the hug ended. Her husband had managed to curb her outright complaining, but there was no stopping the woman's valid criticism of the condition of the house and its furnishings. She started with the size of the table they were eating at before moving on to the quality of the plates and the silverware and the state of the kitchen and the bathrooms...

"Mom, I know it's not like home, but we like it here. We have a lake and kayaks and woods and stuff to do and we're outside most of the time anyway. Besides, it's only for the summer." The almost pleading tone in Audrey's voice did not go unnoticed by her mother.

"Point taken," said Mrs. Conroy in a business-like manner, but her tone did seem to soften. "We have a beautiful view and tons of great food. I can't wait to explore the area. What would you guys like to do this weekend?" For all her talk about relaxing and reading, the woman was obviously gearing up for a busy weekend.

"I for one want to give this kayaking a try," said Mr. Conroy. "And maybe get in a little golf or tennis. Any takers?"

"Dad, I'll take you kayaking!" Audrey jumped at the chance to spend some quality time with her father. Almost as if to avoid hurting her mother's feelings, she quickly added, "Mom, there's this really cool house across the lake I want to show you. I'm dying to see the inside of it."

"Sounds interesting," agreed Mrs. Conroy. "You know how much I love houses."

"I wouldn't mind some golf myself," said Mr. Harris. "Dakota, are you up for it? Who knows? You might even like it."

"If you men decide to go golfing, we girls can do some shopping." Mrs. Conroy sounded quite pleased with her own suggestion. "We passed an antique shop on the way in that looked really interesting and I would bet the prices for antiques out here are a lot better than back in Dunellon." She looked surprised when everybody at the table started laughing.

"Mom, since when do you even look at prices?" Audrey asked in a gentle tone. "I'm definitely up for shopping. Do you think there's a mall around here?" Audrey shared her mother's shopping gene.

Dakota winked at his sister. Erin had been on a few shopping expeditions with the Conroy women and she knew all too well what she was in for.

"I'll make sure to wear sensible shoes," Erin said quietly. Audrey smiled at her, glad that her friend was not automatically excluding herself from what Erin considered another shopping ordeal.

"Well, if you guys didn't save room for Nora's chocolate cake, it's your own fault," Mr. Conroy announced as he started to clear the table. "I warned everybody."

"We'll do the dishes Mr. Conroy," Erin said, getting up and taking the dishes from his hand. "Come on, you two," she prompted when Audrey and Dakota remained seated at the table. "Why don't you guys walk down to the dock? We'll bring the cake. It's nice to sit down there in the evening." When the adults started down the path to the dock, Sadie and Patches seemed torn, but finally decided to stay in the house with the leftovers until Erin shooed them away.

Chapter 8

The Perrys

Erin returned from her solo walk on Saturday morning to find everybody on the deck eating breakfast and listening to Mrs. Conroy complain about how the loud window air conditioning units had kept her awake most of the night. There was a break in the conversation when Erin joined them and exactly in that short, quiet moment they all heard the disgusting sound of a man coughing up phlegm and spitting.

"Ewww, gross!" Audrey exclaimed.

"What on earth was that?" Mrs. Conroy had the same look of disgust on her face as her daughter.

"It's those fishermen," Dakota explained. "They're out there every day in the same spot under the trees." As an afterthought, he added, "They're not very friendly either."

"I guess that's one disadvantage of being right on the water. Certainly never occurred to me when we rented this house," said Mr. Conroy thoughtfully. "Speaking of being on the water, is my favorite daughter taking me kayaking this morning? I think our camp director has a lot of activities planned for today." He smiled at his wife when he said that.

"Let's go!" Audrey answered and jumped up immediately. The girl adored her father. "All the gear is under the deck. It'll only take a minute to get it. We can paddle across the lake!"

"I'll get us a tee time for this afternoon, Alan" offered Mr. Harris. "Dakota, are you up for golf?"

"Sure," the boy replied with a noticeable lack of enthusiasm. He had tried to talk Mr. Conroy and his father into visiting Monticello, but golf had won out with the men. Mr. Harris understood Dakota's love of history, but still found it hard to believe his son wanted to go to work on his day off. The boy probably just wanted Mr. Conroy to see Monticello. Ever since the Conroys had moved to Dunellon, Dakota had been doing lawn work and odd jobs for them and he was almost a part of the family. Even Nora, the Conroy's housekeeper, adored him.

"The game of golf actually has quite an interesting history, son," Mr. Harris said, trying to spark some enthusiasm in Dakota for the classic game. "You might find it more interesting than you think."

"Cody, let's take the dogs for a walk," Erin suggested, rescuing her brother from a lecture by their father about the history of golf. "They'll be in the house all afternoon while we're gone. I can put my sensible shoes on when we get back," she added, smiling at Mrs. Conroy.

As they left the house with the dogs, Erin saw Audrey and her father pushing off from the shore in the kayaks. The boats were wobbling a little, but from a distance it looked like both paddlers had huge grins on their faces. The sight made

Erin smile and she thought again how glad she was to have Audrey as a friend. She wouldn't suffer through an afternoon of shopping for just anybody.

Fortunately for Erin, the Conroy women could not find a mall within a hundred mile radius so they had to settle for the local antique shops, which Erin actually enjoyed. Mrs. Conroy spent a small fortune on totally unnecessary stuff for the lake house and her home in Dunellon. She justified it by saying the BMW was empty. They had delivered all of Nora's food so there was plenty of room in the car for her antique shop finds. Erin and Audrey bought a glass paperweight with a purple and white flower in it for Nora to thank her for all the home cooking she had sent. Mrs. Conroy decided it would be a great idea if they all went out for a nice dinner, no offense to anybody's cooking, so she asked every single store owner what they thought was the best restaurant in the area.

The shoppers and the golfers arrived back at the house almost simultaneously. Before anybody could share stories about their day, Mrs. Conroy asked her husband to make reservations for dinner at the Clifton House, which several shop owners had recommended. Mr. Harris silently questioned the practicality of going out to eat when they had so much food at home, but he knew better than to say anything. Besides, he knew Nora's cooking would not go to waste with three teenagers to feed.

After a quick, but totally refreshing swim, they fed the dogs and piled into the BMW to satisfy Mrs. Conroy's desire for a gourmet dinner.   The Clifton House sat on top of a hill surrounded by gardens as beautiful as those at Monticello. It was an old country inn with a history of its own from the Jefferson era, and most importantly for Mrs. Conroy, a four star kitchen.   The   owners   had   managed   to   add   modern conveniences without destroying the quaint historical features of the restaurant, giving it a very sophisticated, yet comfortable feel. None of them were disappointed, which was saying a lot considering the many differences in their individual appetites. Between the six of them they sampled most of the menu while they shared stories about their afternoon golf and shopping outings.

As they were leaving the restaurant, Audrey spotted the twins from the big house across the lake having dinner with their parents. Of course, she gave them a big wave in spite of the nudge she got from Erin. And of course Audrey's parents were curious about any boys their daughter knew, so Mrs. Conroy introduced herself and the two groups ended up having coffee and dessert on the restaurant patio overlooking the beautiful lantern-filled gardens.

It had cooled off enough so that it was almost pleasant outside and most of the group enjoyed themselves, but Erin couldn't wait to leave. She didn't care much for the twins' company, and she had the impression her father felt the same way because he sat politely, but silently, after introducing himself. Mr. Perry, the twins' father, was a marketing manager for an international software company and when he talked about corporate America and global markets with Mr. Conroy, it was like a language nobody else understood. Mrs. Conroy discovered the twins' mother shared her passion for interior decorating and the two women talked like they had known each other for years.

Audrey and Dakota talked to the twins for a while, but Dakota quickly found he didn't have much in common with the boys besides the lake. David and Daniel went to a private boarding school in Washington, DC, and their world was very different than Dakota's in many ways. When Dakota started talking about history and working at Monticello, the boys were clearly bored, and when the twins started name dropping about people in the city, Dakota returned the favor. Erin didn't even attempt to tell them about the albino. Audrey, however, could have chatted forever about D.C and when the adults finally stood up to leave, two of their three children wasted no time in following them.

"That was absolutely delightful," said Mrs. Conroy on the way home. "What a lovely restaurant - and I'm so glad we met our neighbors from across the lake. Those boys seem very nice, Audrey, and their manners are impeccable. Mrs. Perry told me there's a regatta on the lake tomorrow morning and she invited us for brunch, so you just might get to see the inside of the house. Apparently they have a brunch every year on the day of the regatta – it's some kind of family tradition. I'm sure it will be very nice. I'm glad I brought some decent clothes."

"Did you hear what Mr. Perry said about the man who owns our rental house?" Mr. Conroy asked his wife. "He said somebody's been trying to buy it for years, but the owner won't sell. Says he wants to keep it for his retirement, so my guess is he's probably waiting until then to renovate. I can't think of any other reason why somebody would let that place get so run down. The owner loves the house, but his wife hates it, so that's why they rent it out. Mr. Perry said the man is a fool, at least from a business point of view, because somebody has been offering him a lot of money for that house."

"I wonder what it's worth," mused Mrs. Conroy. "It would be a huge undertaking to renovate that place." She paused before adding, "But it does have potential, and it might even be fun..." Nobody else seemed too interested in the topic and it was quiet in the car for the rest of the drive home.

As soon as they got back to the lake house, the parents headed for bed and the teens raced down to the dock with the dogs for a nighttime swim. Dakota's attempts to teach Sadie to jump off the dock into the water were still unsuccessful, but his efforts provided some great late night entertainment for the girls. It was awesome to swim in the dark and it made the humid night air a bit more bearable, but by the time they hiked up the path to the house they were all hot and sticky again. The loud window

AC units made it hard for everybody to sleep, but nobody wanted to turn them off.

Dakota thought it would be cool to kayak across the lake to the Perry's regatta brunch, but he changed his mind in the morning when he saw all the sailboats on the water. He was smart enough to know his limits with a kayak. Erin had visions of her brother trying to maneuver between the racing boats, disrupting the whole regatta. She was glad he decided not to paddle over, but the image in her mind of Dakota kayaking through the middle of the racing boats put a smile on her face.

Mr. Harris declined to go, claiming that the beautiful Clifton House was a perfect fit for his historical fiction story and he wanted to write about it while it was fresh in his mind. Erin would have preferred to stay with her father, but she was a little curious about the swanky brunch at the house across the lake and Audrey really wanted her to go. Even though everyone assured Erin she looked fine in her summer skirt and low heels, she still felt rather unsophisticated compared to Audrey and Mrs. Conroy, who were both perfectly dressed and totally self-assured. Erin still hadn't learned how to be comfortable in formal settings, but she was slowly improving.

Her brother, however, was not at all self-conscious because he pretty much didn't care what other people thought of him. Erin made Dakota promise not to desert her at the party, knowing full well it meant she would be subjected to his endless discussions about history with anybody who would listen. Sometimes she envied him his passion. At any rate, she was certain being with Dakota would be better than trying to keep up with any of the Conroys at a party.

The lawn was already filled with guests by the time the little group arrived. It looked like something out of a fashion magazine to Erin and she couldn't believe how beautiful everybody looked. Even the people wearing jeans looked like movie stars. Erin decided it was because they paid so much attention to details – every hair was in place, make-up was perfect, shoes looked new and all their clothes fit perfectly. There was something about the confident way those people carried themselves that made Erin feel really awkward, especially in her K-Mart skirt.

Mrs. Perry invited them inside for a tour of the house which turned out to be even more impressive than Audrey and Erin had imagined. The huge open living area overlooking the lake offered a fantastic view of the water from every window and had obviously cost a fortune to decorate. The style of the house was an eclectic mish-mash of antiques and unique pieces pulled together with Mrs. Perry's decorating skills. It was stunning, unique, and yet comfortable and lived-in all at the same time. Even Mrs. Conroy was impressed.

After the tour of the house, Mrs. Perry turned her younger guests over to her sons who invited them out to see what they called "the dog house." Mr. and Mrs. Conroy joined the party on the lawn while Erin, Audrey and Dakota followed the twins into a kennel which was the size of a small house and cleaner than most homes people live in. There must have been twenty dogs in the cages lining both walls and every single one of them sat or stood patiently when they saw the twins. Those dogs were well-behaved.

The twins were giving what Erin considered a condescending speech on dog breeding when she spotted the dog with the lightning bolt on his forehead. He was standing quietly in the corner of his cage like the others, but he looked awful. One of his ears was all chewed up, he had cuts all over his body and it looked like he was having trouble standing.

"What happened to Harry? Erin blurted out.

"Who's Harry?" asked Daniel, the more outgoing twin.

Erin blushed and pointed to the injured dog to explain what she was talking about. "When I saw him the other day that name just popped into my head. You know – because of the lightning bolt on his forehead." She was still blushing and she felt uncomfortable asking more questions, but she continued out of concern for the dog. "What happened to him? He looks terrible."

"He got into a little fight, that's all," Daniel said in his condescending tone. "He needs to learn how to take better care of himself." The boy acted as if nothing was wrong.

"Poor thing," Erin said, moving towards the cage with the injured dog.

"Please don't do that," David spoke up, not unkindly. "We spend a lot of money to train these dogs and it just confuses them when strangers try to be friendly. Don't worry about him – he'll be fine." His tone was not as condescending as his brother's, but he definitely meant what he said. He stood between Erin and the dog, waiting for her to move away.

Erin stopped in her tracks and turned to Audrey and Dakota for support, but they were already leaving the kennel with Daniel. She cast a concerned glance in the direction of Harry's cage before slowly joining the others. Erin did not enjoy the rest of the party because she could not stop thinking about the injured dog. She didn't even watch the regatta.

"You're exaggerating, Erin," insisted Dakota when his sister said she thought Harry was being abused. "Mr. Perry breeds those dogs and I'm sure he does it for money. He's too good a businessman to let anything happen to his investment. Besides," he continued, "I bet those dogs get better care than most people. Those kennels were amazing."

"You just don't like the twins," Audrey added, taking Dakota's side in the discussion. "I don't think they were being condescending. That's just the way they are. Maybe you misinterpreted their tone." When Audrey saw the upset look on her friend's face, she softened a little. "Okay, maybe they are a little bit snooty, but I'm sure that's just because their parents are rich. You're still going to their Fourth of July party, aren't you?"

Audrey looked a little worried when she asked her friend that question. She did not want to go without her.

Erin thought for a moment before she answered. "OK, but if I don't have a good time at the party, I'm not going over there anymore. I honestly don't understand what you see in those boys." Erin turned away from Audrey and muttered under breath, "at least I'll be able to check on Harry at the party."

Chapter 9

Tommy

After Mr. and Mrs. Conroy left, the residents of the lake house settled back into their summer routine, with one minor change – Old Blue. All of them were grateful to Audrey's parents for bringing the car to the lake house even though Dakota was the only one of the teenagers who had a license. He drove the ancient little blue VW Beetle to work every morning and was usually home just in time for lunch. Every day without fail, he regaled them with stories about Thomas Jefferson or Monticello or some historical tidbit about central Virginia.   Who would have thought mowing the historical presidential lawn could be so exciting? Afternoons were spent running errands for Mr. Harris, playing miniature golf, swimming, kayaking or exploring the area. The teens went to the country store for ice cream so often that Heather, the real estate agent's daughter behind the counter, knew their orders by heart.

Erin walked in the nature preserve almost every morning while her father wrote, and Audrey read or watched TV. There was something magical about the forest in the early morning and Erin was hooked on being part of it. She saw regular deer (that's what she called the ones that weren't albinos) almost every day. They were often in the front yard of the lake house, which drove Sadie and Patches crazy, but Erin rarely saw the albino. The few times she did see the beautiful white fawn, she found herself wishing that Audrey and Dakota were there to see it, too. She realized the experience would be even more magical if she could share it.

Early one morning before the heavy fog had lifted from the lake, Erin saw Tommy sitting alone by the side of the trail in the nature preserve. She started to say hello, but right before she opened her mouth, she realized he was intent on watching something in the woods. *Maybe it's the albino*, thought Erin as she cautiously made her way along the path to where the boy was sitting. Tommy looked up and gave Erin one of his great smiles, but he didn't seem at all surprised to see her. He motioned silently for her to sit and it was the most natural thing in the world for Erin to plop down next to him in the middle of the woods. Sure enough, he was watching the albino selectively pick leaves off the lower branches of trees about 10 yards away. The shy creature looked up and froze for a moment when Erin appeared, but didn't run away, and soon went back to picking leaves off the low hanging branches.

The boy and the girl sat silently, side by side, watching the pink ears and white face bob up and down for what seemed liked hours. They didn't talk, but every now and then one of them turned to the other and smiled. Erin was amazed at how comfortable she felt sitting there with Tommy and she was disappointed when the albino leisurely wandered off into the woods, still picking at leaves as it went.

"Lucy," said Tommy with a grin on his face, "is amazing!"

Erin smiled and felt herself blushing. She couldn't believe Tommy remembered the name she had given the albino. That boy was so nice. He helped her up and started to walk home with her and before they knew it, they were at the lake house.

"Come on in and meet my father," Erin invited.

Tommy hesitated, and Erin recognized the same reluctance she often felt when she met new people.

"He's a pretty nice guy. He hasn't murdered any teenagers yet," she said smiling. "Come on in for a minute."

Sadie and Patches immediately made Tommy feel welcome with one of their more enthusiastic dog greetings. Erin was certain they sensed what a good person he was and they certainly must have realized that he adored dogs. Tommy relaxed noticeably with the dogs circling around him, nudging him for pets and possibly treats.

"Hi Tommy," came a voice from the couch. Audrey's head popped up from the book she was reading and she smiled at both of them. "Did you guys see the albino in the woods today?"

"Yeah – she's amazing," Tommy repeated his statement from earlier.

"We watched her for the longest time. I wish you had been there," Erin told Audrey, and she meant it.

"Well, if you hadn't left so early, I might have gone with you. What time did you get up?"

Before Erin had time to tease her friend about sleeping in every day, Mr. Harris appeared in the living room. Tommy separated himself from the dogs and walked over to introduce himself. Erin knew her father would be impressed with the boy's good manners - she just hoped he would be able to overlook Tommy's straggly long hair and scruffy appearance.

"Nice to meet you, son," said Mr. Harris, and turned to his daughter after shaking the boy's hand. "How was your walk, Erin? Pretty morning for it."

Tommy ended up staying for a while. When Erin asked if he wanted to go kayaking, he jumped at the chance. He said he had only been kayaking a few times in his life and he was eager to try it again. Audrey couldn't believe he lived in a lake community year-round and his family didn't have a boat. Of course she had to share her thoughts out loud with the others.

"We can't afford one," Tommy explained without any sign of embarrassment, which really impressed Erin. "It's just my Mom and me ... and the dogs, but it's OK. I can still go swimming and sometimes I go out in friends' boats."

"Do you know the twins across the lake?" Audrey asked. "They said they have a couple of boats."

"Let's get the kayaks on the water before it gets too hot," Erin interrupted, changing the subject. She was pretty certain Tommy didn't hang out with the two rich boys who lived in a mansion and went to boarding school in DC. "Are you coming, Audrey? We can take turns."

"You guys go ahead. I'm almost done with my book and I really want to finish it. I'll come down later." Audrey disappeared back into the couch with her book.

It turned out Tommy was a natural in the kayak and Erin had a hard time keeping up with him. They started out paddling close to shore and Tommy kept looking up into the woods like he was searching for the albino.

"Look at that one leaf floating on the water," Erin said, pointing. "It's amazing how clean this lake is. I hardly ever see any trash or..."

"What are you kids doing here?" a gruff voice cut Erin off in mid-sentence. "You're scaring the fish away with all that splashing." The men in the fishing boat seemed to appear out of nowhere.

"We're just kayaking, sir," Tommy paddled his kayak between Erin and the fishing boat, a protective gesture that did not go unnoticed by the girl.

"Well scat!" snapped the second ornery man. "Go paddle somewhere else. This is the best fishing spot on the whole lake and it don't make no sense to waste it on a couple of kids in kayaks."

"Come on, Erin. Let's go," said Tommy, gently pushing Erin's boat out into the deeper water. It was exactly like something Dakota would have done.

"They don't own the lake!" Erin exploded once they were out of earshot from the grumpy old men.

"Sometimes it's just better not to argue, especially with people like that," said Tommy reasonably. "Let them have their spot. There's a whole lake out here and I don't want to be around a couple of grumpy old men anyway."

"They're always rude to us," Erin continued. "Cody said he saw them dragging something up out of the water, but they threw it back in the lake when they saw him. For some reason, I don't think it was a fish," she added abruptly.

"I would stay out of their way if I were you, Erin. I don't know who those men are, but they clearly don't want us around." Tommy turned his boat so he could look directly at Erin. "Promise me you'll keep away from them," he said seriously.

Erin's first reaction was to rebel against Tommy's request. She already had one older brother who told her what to do and she didn't need another one. She tried to choose her words carefully before she answered him because she didn't want to sound rude, but Tommy burst out laughing before she opened her mouth to speak.

"You should see the look on your face! I'm sorry. I wasn't trying to boss you around. I guess I'm kind of used to looking after my Mom." He laughed again. "Some poker face you have!"

Erin's mood changed instantly. She couldn't resist Tommy's laughter. "Race you across the lake!" she challenged and started paddling as hard as she could. Even with a head start Erin came in well behind Tommy, but she was still laughing when they reached the shore.

Tommy spent more and more time at the lake house over the following weeks, and everybody grew to like him. It was his last summer at home before graduating from high school and his mother wanted him to enjoy it, so she had insisted that he didn't work. He did some dog sitting for people at the lake and he did chores around the house to help his mother, but he had a lot of free time and he enjoyed spending it with Erin, Audrey and Dakota.

Mr. Harris liked the boy. Tommy always made of point of asking how the writing was coming along and he provided some interesting facts for Mr. Harris to use in his book. Having grown up in the area, Tommy knew a lot about local history, even though he was not passionate about it like Dakota and Mr. Harris. Tommy wanted to be a veterinarian when he grew up. His passion was animals, especially dogs. What a surprise.

Everybody at the lake knew Tommy. Well, almost everybody. Audrey asked the twins about him and they had no idea who he was. For some reason, Audrey was determined to get Tommy invited to the twins' Fourth of July party and she used all her persuasive talents to make it happen. Erin did not think it was good idea because she felt uncomfortable around the snooty boys and she didn't want to put Tommy in the same position, even though she was pretty sure he could take care of himself. He was obviously shy, but he seemed to handle most situations quite well.

Audrey was proud of herself when she finally convinced the twins to invite the local boy to their party and she couldn't wait to tell Tommy he was invited to a big Fourth of July bash. She got the opportunity when Dakota offered to treat the girls to ice cream at the country store (again) on a Saturday afternoon. There was a heap of skateboards by the front door when they pulled up in Old Blue. Tommy was inside with his friends.

"Tommy, want to go to a party?" Audrey didn't even say hello first. She just jumped right in.

The boy was standing at the counter with a strawberry ice cream cone, talking to Heather. The two of them turned their heads in unison and there was something very cozy about the way they looked together. Erin felt a pang of something she couldn't quite place, but she knew it was something uncomfortable. *Is Heather his girlfriend?* The thought flashed uninvited into her mind and she had a hard time shaking it. She just hoped she hadn't asked the question out loud.

"Hi guys," said Tommy to the group, but his smile was for Erin. This time it was Heather who had a questioning look on her face. "Are you having a party, Audrey?" she asked.

"No, it's the twins across the lake. You know that big house across from ours? They're having a Fourth of July party and I got Tommy an invitation," Audrey looked proud of herself for a brief moment, but Tommy's response changed that.

The boy glanced quickly at Heather, who flashed him a smile. Erin noticed how well they understood each other without saying a word.

"Thanks, but I can't. There's a bunch of us who always watch the fireworks together on the Fourth," Tommy explained. "Sounds like fun, though." He was polite, but he showed no enthusiasm and Erin was sure the party didn't really sound like fun to him at all.

"Are they the dog breeders?" one of the skateboarders asked. "They don't usually hang out with us." He didn't sound upset about it. "Everybody says they have some beautiful dogs, though, supposedly champion show dogs." He turned to his friend, "Tommy you should go just to see the dogs."

"Exactly what I was thinking!" Audrey said triumphantly. "Come on, Tommy." Yes, Audrey was persistent.

"Go ahead if you want," Heather encouraged him, and Erin felt that uncomfortable pang again. She needed to talk to Audrey about this.

"This is probably my last fireworks here for a while. I kind of like our tradition." Tommy turned to Erin and gave her a big smile. Erin could not believe how confused she felt. "You're welcome to come with us. We climb up on those big rocks at the end of the lake and the view is great." Then he turned to Audrey, laughing, "It's not fancy, but it's fun."

"Erin – don't you dare say yes!" Audrey must have read her friend's mind. "You promised you would go to this party with me, remember?"

"I know, I know. Don't worry. I'll go to the party," Erin promised. At that moment the last thing she wanted to do was go hang out with Tommy and Heather. "Can we get our ice cream now?" she asked, changing the subject. She was ready to get out of there.

"Do you guys want to go play some putt-putt?" Tommy certainly didn't seem to notice Erin's discomfort. "We're on our way over there now." He asked the question to Erin, Audrey and Dakota as a group, but he was only looking at Erin.

"Yeah, that sounds great!" answered Dakota, his usual enthusiastic self. "We'll get our ice cream and meet you there. We know where it is." He paused for a minute before turning back to Tommy with a questioning look on his face, "Do you guys have a car? I don't think we would all fit in the old Beetle."

"We'll be there before you are," Tommy said, moving towards the door with his friends. Erin watched them heading off on their skateboards while she waited for her ice cream cone. She was really confused.

"One chocolate, one coconut, and one mint chocolate chip coming right up," Heather said cheerfully as she slid open the cover to the freezer bin. The girl showed absolutely no sign of being uncomfortable around Erin. "Watch out, Tommy's pretty good at putt-putt," she warned them with her pretty smile. "If you guys change your minds about the Fourth of July, you're welcome to join us on the rocks. I love to watch the fireworks from up there." She gave Dakota a big smile as she handed him his chocolate ice cream cone, and it was Audrey's turn to wonder what the heck was going on.

They took their time eating the ice cream, certain the boys on skateboards could use a head start. Dakota chatted with Heather while Erin and Audrey ate in silence, their wide eyes communicating volumes without words.

"Was she flirting with you?" Erin asked her brother when they got in the car. Audrey said nothing.

"I don't think so," answered Dakota matter-of-factly. "She's just friendly. She's like that with everybody." Audrey rolled her eyes at Erin.

Whether or not Heather was a flirt might have been questionable, but she was certainly right about Tommy's miniature golfing talent. The skateboarders were waiting with grins on their faces when Old Blue pulled up at the putt-putt course, but nobody said a word about how they had gotten there so quickly. Because there were so many of them, they had to split up into two groups and Tommy beat them all. He played with Erin and Audrey and one of his skateboard friends, and Dakota played with the rest of the guys.

It turned out Audrey was also pretty good at the game. She was competitive about most things and she was the only one who really challenged Tommy. It was a blast. It took Erin all of five minutes to feel comfortable around Tommy again and she would have played another round if the skateboarders had been able to stay, but they couldn't. Before they all split up, Audrey proclaimed that Tommy just had a lucky day and confidently said she would cream him in a rematch, a challenge the boy readily accepted. He grinned at Erin when he said that.

On the way home Audrey kept talking about putt-putt and the skateboarders. "You know, for a bunch of scruffy looking guys, they're not bad," she said. Erin just smiled at her friend.

When Erin looked out the window the next morning, her heart almost stopped. The albino was lying in the side yard in the middle of all the leaves, looking like she owned the place. A huge smile spread across the girl's face as she stood at the upstairs window, mesmerized by the beautiful creature. *Audrey,* she thought suddenly, and ran down the hall to wake her friend.

"Lucy's in the yard," she said, gently shaking Audrey's shoulder. "Wake up!"

"Who? What time is it?" Audrey was definitely not a morning person. She propped herself up on one elbow and tried to figure out what was going on. "What are you talking about?" she asked, still half asleep.

"The albino – she's in the yard." Erin started dragging Audrey out of bed, but suddenly Audrey caught on and jumped up, wide awake. Patches lifted her head up from her nest at Audrey's feet, but decided to stay in bed.

"Go look out my window, but you have to be quiet. I'll go get Cody and Dad." Erin ran as quietly as she could down the stairs, hoping and praying Sadie would sleep right through this.

The albino was still there after Erin woke her father and brother. Mr. Harris's bedroom had a side window directly below his daughter's window and they had the same view, so everybody crowded around it to watch Erin's magical creature in the yard. Audrey joined them after a few minutes with wide eyes and her camera.

"She's so pretty, Erin," Audrey said. "I think I got some good pictures from upstairs, but they're kind of far away."

"I think she looks like something out of a fairy tale, like a unicorn," Erin's voice was full of awe. "I'm so glad you guys finally got to see her."

"It looks like a goat," Dakota declared. When his sister hit him on the back, he laughingly defended himself. "Really, it does, doesn't it Dad?"

"It's an albino, that's for sure. Look at those pink ears and pink eyes. Sometimes white deer are mistaken for albinos." Mr. Harris had a tendency to turn everything into a lecture. "I can see why you've gone looking for her every morning, Erin. She's neat."

When Sadie and Patches finally decided to investigate why everybody was huddled around the window, the fawn picked up her head as if she sensed the dogs. For a moment, the pink eyes stared directly at the window, and then the albino/unicorn/goat bolted off into the woods.

"I am so glad you guys finally got to see her!" Erin said again.

Chapter 10

Fourth of July – The Races

Mr. and Mrs. Conroy came back to the lake for the Fourth of July weekend with another trunk full of Nora's cooking. Much to everyone's relief, there was a break in the weather and the window air conditioners were not necessary. Those living in the house had gotten used to the noisy things, but everybody knew Mrs. Conroy would complain if the rackety clatter kept her awake again. Actually, it would have taken more than a little complaining to put a damper on the good spirits in the lake house. The teens were excited about the fireworks, the races, the twins' party (Audrey) and all the other stuff going on for the holiday weekend.

"Did you know that Thomas Jefferson died on the Fourth of July?" Dakota asked at dinner on Friday evening, in between bites of spaghetti with Nora's awesome homemade sauce and meatballs.

"Yes, because you already told us about 700 times," answered Audrey, rolling her eyes at Erin.

"What year?" asked Mr. Conroy, showing genuine interest.

"1826, exactly fifty years after we declared our independence," Dakota offered eagerly, and the girls were certain the dinner conversation was headed for another history lesson. It happened almost every night with Dakota and Mr. Harris, and Mr. Conroy's presence would surely seal the deal. The girls usually listened patiently for a while, but they had their limits.

Mrs. Conroy saved the day. "What are the plans for tomorrow? I would love to get some tennis in. This weather is heavenly."

"There's a 5k race around the golf course in the morning, then in the afternoon there's a swimming race across the lake and a bunch of other stuff at the clubhouse," Audrey explained, grateful for her mother's question. "Anybody want to do the 5k with me? I don't think I want to swim across the lake, but it would be fun to watch - and there's a sand sculpture competition, too."

"I'd rather go for my walk in the woods in the morning, but I'll go down to the beach with you in the afternoon," Erin was over her ear infection. "Cody, are you running or swimming?" Erin asked her brother. "Tommy said he would be there," she added quietly.

"Let's all do both races," suggested Dakota. "It'll be fun, even if we come in last."

Everybody answered him at once and it took a while to figure out who would do what, but at least it was a lively discussion. Erin could not be talked out of her morning walk in the woods, but all the others agreed to do the 5k, and Mr.

Conroy tentatively agreed to the swim if he wasn't too beat. Dakota wanted to compete in both races, even though he knew he wouldn't win either one of them. He was more of a football type athlete, not a racer, but he could hold his own in any sporting event and he loved anything outdoors.

They were making friendly wagers on the races while devouring Nora's delicious strawberry cheesecake when a voice called up from the water, "Audrey, Erin! Are you there?" Everybody on the deck turned to see where the voice had come from, but they couldn't make out much through the trees.

"It's the twins," Audrey said as she stood up. "They must be down at the dock. Come on Erin -let's go see what they want."

Erin got up, but took her time because she was not exactly in a hurry to see their visitors. When she finally got down to the dock, Daniel was sitting in his kayak chatting up a storm with Audrey while David sat quietly next to his brother. *I thought you liked fast boats*, thought Erin. She nodded hello, and just let the two talkers continue their conversation about the party and their plans for the Fourth.

"We're having a band and everything and at least 50 kids. You guys could kayak over," Daniel suggested. He actually sounded pretty excited for a cool snobby twin. "The party is for us, but our parents told us to invite your parents if they want to come."

"I think our folks want some adult company. It doesn't take long for them to get bored around a group of kids," David made his quiet contribution to the conversation.

"Cool, I'll ask them. Are you guys doing any races tomorrow?" Audrey loved chatting.

"No, that stuff's pretty boring," Daniel responded. "Besides, we don't really know anybody here."

"Neither do we, but we're still going – and I think it will be fun," Audrey countered.

"We don't really hang out with the people who live here," David said with finality.

Erin had enough. "See you guys tomorrow," she said turning to leave. "I'm going to take the dogs out. Are you coming Audrey?"

"I'll be up in a minute," Audrey replied distractedly. As Erin made her way up the path to the house, she heard Audrey ask a barrage of questions about the party and who would be there and what they had planned and what she should wear. The twins answered her as fast as they could, laughing loudly and assuring her it would be an awesome party. All three of them seemed to enjoy the conversation. Erin was dreading the party.

The cool evening air was refreshing, even a little chilly. Erin smiled when she got back up to the house and saw the others gathered around the fire pit. It was the first time they had made a fire at the lake house, and Dakota was eagerly adding wood to the little fire.   "I'll go get the marshmallows," Erin volunteered, ready for any distraction that would put the thought of the snooty twins out of her mind.   Audrey didn't say a word about the boys when she finally came back up the path.   The two girls understood each other very well.

It was cozy and peaceful sitting around the fire watching the stars come out.   Even the dogs settled down to enjoy the cool night air.   Mrs. Conroy surprised everyone by pointing out a bunch of constellations, and they even saw a few shooting stars.   Of course, the guys eventually got their history conversation, but nobody else in the group minded.   It was peaceful just to sit and look at the stars with voices in the background.   All of them were reluctant to go to bed and they stayed up way too late.

The Fourth of July was just as cool as the preceding day – perfect for a 5k race, and also perfect for seeing an albino deer.   Erin returned from her morning walk with a satisfied smile on her face, eager to share some unicorn magic with the others, but she had to wait.   The 5k group had just returned from their race and Erin was bombarded with stories before she could tell them she had seen Lucy.

"Sounds like you guys had a good time," she said with a satisfied smile still on her face.   "Who won the race?"

They all answered at once, telling their own versions of how the race went. Each of them had finished the 5k, but at very different times.

"Tommy won," Audrey said, sounding surprised. "He finished first and nobody was even close to him. He was amazing!"

Erin felt a flush of pride when she heard that.

"I was almost dead last, but I did it," said Mr. Harris proudly. "I came in with a bunch of grey haired folks who were in better shape than me," he added with a big laugh. "Did Nora send any of her biscuits this time? I'm starving." Mrs. Conroy nodded and starting getting breakfast ready, which Erin greatly appreciated. It was a treat to have someone else put a meal on the table, especially since she knew Mrs. Conroy did not cook very often, even in her own home - that was Nora's responsibility.

After a huge breakfast of homemade biscuits and sausage gravy, the teens sat on the dock with their parents and the dogs and watched the lake fill up with boats. It was quite a contrast to the quiet scene they had been enjoying for the past month and it was fun to watch. A lot of people had come to the lake for the holiday weekend, making for a festive atmosphere on the water.

"Who's swimming across the lake with me?" Cody asked.

"Not me," answered his father promptly.

"Sorry, but I guess I'm out, too, Dakota," Mr. Conroy apologized. "I don't have enough energy to swim across the lake *and* beat my wife at tennis. She showed me up in the 5k, but I'll get even with her on the tennis court."

"We'll see who beats whom," Mrs. Conroy retorted. "Would you care to place a small wager? How about brunch at the Clifton House tomorrow morning?" It was a pretty silly bet, considering Mr. Conroy would take her anyway.

"Deal," answered her husband promptly. He knew better than to try to talk her out of a bet.

"I'm not swimming, but I want to watch the race and see the sand sculptures," Erin told her brother.

"We can be your cheerleaders," Audrey chimed in. "Tommy said he won the swim race last year. It would be cool if he won the 5k and the lake race today." She smiled at Erin, "He seems pretty determined. Oh I forgot to tell you – he asked where you were this morning."

Erin felt herself blushing and was relieved when Dakota got up to go. "Are you guys ready to head down to the beach?" he asked. "I want to see the sand sculptures before the race." The girls quickly joined him. Audrey practiced cheerleading as they headed up the path to the house and Dakota struck muscle man poses. Erin didn't pay any attention to either of them - she was thinking about seeing Tommy.

The beach was packed with people signing up for the race and others milling around to look at the sand sculptures.

Erin was admiring a giant sea turtle carved out of sand when Tommy appeared beside her, all smiles. She turned to say hello and immediately noticed he didn't look as scruffy as usual. He had gotten a haircut. When Erin suddenly realized she was staring at his face, she quickly looked away, feeling her face turn beet red. She pretended to examine the sand sculpture at her feet.

"Where were you this morning?" he asked. "I thought you would be at the race."

"I went for my morning walk in the woods – I saw Lucy again!" Erin relaxed a little bit. It was strange that Tommy made her feel so uncomfortable and so comfortable at the same time. "Congratulations on winning the race," she added. "Audrey said you were amazing."

"Well, I wouldn't go that far, but I'm glad I won," Tommy said modestly. "I hope I win the swim race, too. I think that would be cool." He managed to sound excited and proud of himself without bragging. *No small feat*, thought Erin.

"Well good luck," said Erin, and she meant it. "Dakota's swimming too, but he promises he won't be a threat to anybody."

"I heard that," Dakota said, appearing at his sister's side. "And unfortunately it's true," he laughed. "Hi Tommy - good job this morning and good luck with the swim, too. I hope you win," Dakota was enthusiastic and sincere. "I have Old Blue here. Do you want to ride over to the start with me? I think they're lining up over there." The race started on the other side of the lake and finished at the main beach where the sand sculptures were.

"Sure," Tommy answered. "Heather was going to drive me over, but I'd rather go with you. She can be a little too enthusiastic at times and I think I'd rather have some peace and quiet before the race. I'll tell her to drive you back after the race to get your car." Erin wished both of them good luck and called after her brother, "Where's your cheerleader, Cody?"

"She's over by the finish line with Heather," he shouted back, pointing to the crowd gathered at the edge of the lake.

"Hey Erin, I need a cheerleader, too!" Tommy yelled. Erin smiled back at him and was still smiling when she joined Audrey and Heather. The three girls stood on the beach, watching the burst of activity as the judges circled the sand sculptures and the swim race officials cordoned off a finish line a few yards above the water's edge.

"Hi Erin," Heather greeted warmly. "I'm glad you guys came. This is really fun – you'll love it. Did you run the 5k? I missed it, which is too bad because I would have liked to see Tommy win."

Erin noticed for the first time how really pretty Heather was. She had short, curly blond hair and big green eyes and a friendly way about her. For the second time in a matter of minutes, Erin blushed as she realized she was looking intently at another person. She started to answer the girl's question, but

Audrey jumped in to give a full report of the morning race, which was fine with Erin. Sometimes it was just easier for her to let Audrey do the talking.

A loud horn sounded and a voice announced the three-minute warning before the start of the race. The girls could see the swimmers lined up on the beach on the far side of the lake, but it was hard to tell who was who. There must have been over a hundred swimmers of all ages, stretching and talking and jockeying for position. Erin guessed it was about ¾ of a mile from shore to shore and she was glad she wasn't in that mass of people about to take the plunge.

"I think that's Cody!" Audrey shouted and pointed to the left of the pack. She was trying to photograph all the stages of the race.

"There's Tommy right out in front," Heather said proudly. "I hope he wins. He's a great swimmer."

"There's Jamie – remember him, Audrey?" Erin asked. "He gave us that kayak lesson when we first got here. He's out in front of the swimmers in that red kayak, probably in case somebody needs help."

"They're starting!" Heather shouted at the sound of another burst from the horn. "Can you see Tommy?"

At first it was hard to pick anybody out of the mass of arms and heads plunging into the water, but the stronger swimmers in the pack quickly pulled away, leaving the slower ones behind. Gradually the girls were able to make out individual people, but it was still hard to recognize who they were because all they could see were little heads bobbing up and down in the water and arms churning everywhere. It was a cool scene and Audrey got some great shots of it.

"Look – Jamie's rescuing somebody!" Audrey exclaimed, clicking away with her camera. The girls watched along with the other captivated spectators as the little red kayak maneuvered in between the swimmers to a pair of arms signaling for help in the water. The man in the kayak threw a life preserver on a rope to the outstretched arms and towed the swimmer safely to a rescue boat. Once the swimmer was safely in the boat, the crowd on shore started cheering while Jamie headed back to the swimmers, who by this time were spread out halfway across the lake.

"Do you see Tommy?" asked Heather eagerly. The girls searched the water for signs of the two boys they knew.

"There's Cody – way off to the left," Erin said. "He's about halfway across the lake. Can you guys see him?"

"I see him," stated Heather. "He's in the front half of the pack - that's pretty good."

"I see him, too!" exclaimed Audrey. "And look – Tommy's way up front with two other guys, but I can't tell if he's in second or third place from here."

"He has a shot at winning this. Look – he's pulling ahead!" Heather started cheering and whistling for Tommy.

"I hope he doesn't push too hard," Erin said. "They still have a ways to go and it looks like the other two guys are keeping right up with him."

"Tommy can do it," said Heather with confidence. "He can do whatever he puts his mind to."

Erin found herself envious that Heather knew Tommy so well, but she shook it off and cheered with the rest of the onlookers as the three lead swimmers approached the shore. Bit by bit, Tommy managed to widen the gap and take the lead. When he emerged from the water and ran up the roped-off corridor to the finish line, he was met with a huge burst of applause and pats on the back from the people lined up to cheer the racers on. The girls lost sight of Tommy as he was swallowed up by race officials and other swimmers and onlookers and well-wishers.

Erin spotted her brother swimming towards shore and started cheering for him. Within seconds, Audrey and Heather were shouting and yelling along with her as Dakota made his way across the finish line with a big smile on his face. The good-natured crowd applauded every single swimmer as they emerged from the water, with extra loud cheers for the very young and very old who managed to finish the race. Heather knew a lot of the people and kept a running commentary on who was who for Erin and Audrey's benefit. It seemed like the whole town was there.

When the crowd thinned out a little around the swimmers, Tommy and the others posed for photographs alone and with each other. Everybody was smiling and laughing. Erin noticed how Tommy praised the little kids and the elderly who had swum across the lake, and he made sure they got their pictures taken, too. There was something genuinely nice about that boy. Heather ran up to congratulate him with a big hug, and Erin was jolted again by the way she felt when she saw Tommy and Heather together. Audrey noticed both the hug and Erin's reaction to it, but she didn't know what to say. She didn't want to emphasize something that obviously made her friend uncomfortable. Both girls were glad when Dakota appeared.

"Well, I did it," he said, openly proud of himself. "I certainly didn't break any records, but I finished both races. It's kinda cool."

"It is very cool, Cody. You did a great job," praised Audrey, putting her arm across his shoulders. "At least you didn't have to get rescued! Did you see Jamie out there?"

"Yeah, I was going to wave at him, but I figured he'd think I was drowning, so I didn't," Dakota laughed.

"Good job, Cody," praised Erin. "I know I couldn't have done it. I probably wouldn't even have made it off shore with all those people. It looked like a sea of arms and heads out there. I don't know how you guys managed it, but I'm glad Tommy won."

"Me, too," Dakota and Audrey chorused.

"Me, too!" said Tommy, laughing as he appeared with a blue ribbon around his neck and Heather at his side. "For a minute there, I didn't think I was going to win. There was some pretty tough competition this year."

Erin, Audrey and Dakota congratulated the winner, and so did everyone else on the beach who saw him standing there with his friends.

"Let's get out of here," Tommy said. "I'm not used to all this attention. I didn't realize it would be like this."

Heather spoke up. "Dakota, Tommy said you need a ride to the other side of the lake to get your car. I think we can all squeeze in my car – it's not that far," she offered.

"I'd like to walk home," Tommy said. "Even though I'm exhausted, I think I would enjoy a little peace and quiet. Besides, I really don't think anybody wants to get too close to me right now!" He laughed at his own joke. "Hey Erin, if I promise to keep my distance, do you want to walk with me? I know a short cut through the nature preserve."

Erin was taken by surprise at his offer, but she accepted immediately and felt herself blushing again. She did not miss the knowing smile Audrey shot in her direction.

"I'm going with Cody," Audrey said decisively. "That 5k this morning was all the exercise I need for one day. See you at home, Erin. Bye Tommy – congratulations again," she added.

Heather and Dakota and Audrey headed off to the parking lot, leaving Erin alone with Tommy.

Chapter 11

Fourth of July – After the Races

"Come on, Erin. I'll show you a shortcut," Tommy said, signaling with a wave of his arm. Erin followed at his side as he led the way through the thinning crowd on the beach, stopping to acknowledge everybody who congratulated him. At the end of the little street leading away from the beach, Tommy showed her a well-worn path winding between two houses.

"Thanks for walking with me," he said. "I'm really excited about winning those races today, but I can only take so much of all that attention. Isn't it funny how a person can be so competitive and such a loner at the same time?"

"I know what you mean about the attention and the loner part, but I've never been in that position. I guess I'm not very competitive," Erin said. "I think you handled it very well," she added.

"Thanks," Tommy smiled at her again and Erin had to look away. There was that odd mix of feelings again. She felt so comfortable talking to Tommy, but at the same time being around him made her nervous. Whether she liked it or not, she had to admit she had a crush on the boy. Once she acknowledged that to herself, it helped her understand a little bit of what was happening inside her head and she actually started to relax. It was nice to walk and talk with Tommy without other people around and Erin found herself opening up.

She talked about how her mother had died in a plane crash and listened to Tommy talk about his parents' divorce. They talked about their pets and school and the lake and the albino and Tommy's plans for the future, and Erin was totally in her comfort zone by the time they reached Tommy's little house in the overgrown yard.

"Come on in and you can meet my mother," he invited. He laughed out loud when he saw the hesitation in Erin's face, "Don't worry – she's nice. But I have to warn you, she's already heard a lot about you." Tommy gave Erin one of his great smiles and as soon as they climbed the front porch steps they were greeted by a round smiling woman who looked like she had been baking. There was flour all over her apron and patches of the white stuff seemed to float in the air all around her. The smell of something wonderful came pouring out of the house when she opened the front door.

"Hello there! You must be Erin," the woman's voice was just as inviting as the smell of whatever it was she had been baking. "Come on in. Tommy's told me a lot about you," she said, holding the door open for the two teens. "How did you do, Tommy?" she asked, and gave her son a peck on the cheek as he passed her in the doorway.

"He did great. He won!" Erin answered proudly. "How do you do, Mrs. ...." The girl's voice trailed off. "I'm sorry, I don't even know your last name," Erin said, slightly embarrassed.

"Jackson, Amelia Jackson, but you can call me Amy. All Tommy's friends do," the woman was walking back into the house as she talked. "Your timing is perfect. The first batch of chocolate chip cookies just came out of the oven."

"I'll get the milk," Tommy volunteered. He poured three glasses and set them on the kitchen table. "I'll be right back. Just let me change my clothes and then I'll walk you back to your house, Erin." He grabbed two cookies before heading off down the hall. "These are great, Mom," he called back in between bites.

"Are you going to watch the fireworks tonight?" Mrs. Jackson asked Erin, but as soon as she asked the question, the woman jumped up to take another batch of cookies out of the oven. "Peanut butter, my favorite," she said, sampling her work. "Try one while they're still warm," she insisted, setting another plate on the kitchen table in front of Erin.

"These are delicious. Thank you," the girl and the woman chatted for a few minutes until Tommy reappeared. Erin was feeling pretty comfortable sitting there eating cookies with Mrs. Jackson.

"Hey Erin, come on outside and let me introduce you to our dogs," Tommy said. "They're my Mom's favorite children," he added, laughing in his mother's direction. He grabbed a handful of milk bones from a container on the kitchen counter on the way out, and he was immediately surrounded by a pack of dogs when he opened the door. It looked like a familiar routine.

Erin followed cautiously, a little overwhelmed by the number of dogs. "How many dogs do you have?" she asked, trying to sound polite.

"It changes all the time, but today it's only 8," Tommy answered, passing out treats and petting the dogs affectionately. "Mom started taking in strays years ago after my father left and they sort of became our hobby – and our family, too. Sometimes we find homes for them, and if they're really sick or mean we take them to the shelter. All of these guys are sweethearts."

Erin had to agree. The dogs were all shapes and sizes and ages, but every single one of them was friendly.

"It must cost a fortune to keep them all," Erin said, petting the most demanding dogs while she surveyed the pack.

"It does, but Mom and I decided it was something we both wanted to do. We built the kennel out here because we just don't have enough room for this many dogs in the house. I would really like to have one or two in the house, but it wouldn't be fair to the rest," Tommy explained. "You're lucky you have one special dog. Sadie's neat."

"I love her to pieces," Erin admitted, "but I think you're lucky, too. It's kind of cool to have all these dogs at home. No wonder you want to be a vet."

Tommy's mother called out the back door, "Heather's on the phone.   She wants to know what time to pick you up tonight."

"Tell her around 7:30. Thanks, Mom," Tommy answered.

At the mention of Heather's name, Erin felt her mood changing. "I should be getting home. Tell your mother thank you for the cookies. They were great."

"Come on, I'll walk you home. My mother would have a cow if I didn't," Tommy laughed. "You can thank her for the cookies yourself on the way out."

When they went back inside, Mrs. Jackson handed Erin a paper plate full of cookies covered with foil. "I know there are some other teenagers in your house who might enjoy these," she said smiling.

"Thank you, Mrs. Jackson. I might have to hide them from a few adults, too," Erin laughed. "It was nice meeting you."

"Come by anytime, dear," said the friendly woman. "And bring your dog if you like – I'd love to meet her."

"Are you sure you won't come watch the fireworks on the rocks tonight?" Tommy asked Erin on the way home. "It's really cool up there.   Could I bribe you with more cookies?" he laughed.

"No, Audrey would kill me if I didn't go to the party with her," Erin said. "But thanks for the walk and introducing me to your mom and your dogs. They're great."

When Erin and Tommy got to the lake house, Audrey and Dakota spotted them from the deck, calling and waving. Sadie and Patches came bounding out to greet them. Tommy spent a minute petting the dogs and waved up to the other kids on the deck, but he didn't come in. He said he felt badly about leaving his mother alone so much, especially on a holiday.

"I'm sure she understands. She's really nice. Besides, she's not really alone with all those dogs. Tell her thanks again for the cookies. I doubt they'll last long in this house." Erin headed up the path to the house and Tommy started off through the nature preserve.

"Have fun at the party tonight," he called after her, waving. "We'll miss you up on the rocks."

Erin turned around to smile and wave back, glad that nobody could see her face. She really wanted to spend the evening with Tommy, but not if Heather was going to be there. As soon as the thought entered her mind she realized how petty and unkind it was. *What on earth was happening to her?* She needed to talk to Audrey about this.

"Where's Tommy?" asked Dakota when his sister appeared on the deck alone.

"He had to go help his Mom," Erin answered, trying to sound normal. "She sent some homemade cookies for you guys. I would hurry up and get some now because they won't last long. They're really good."

"You met his mother?" Audrey asked incredulously.

"Yes, and his dogs, too," Erin gave Audrey a big smile.

"So what's up with you and Tommy?" asked Dakota. "I mean he's a nice guy and everything, but is there something I should know about?"

"I think you should go teach Sadie to jump off the dock," Audrey intervened. "You said that you'd have her trained by the end of summer and so far I don't see that happening. Erin and I could use a little time alone. Go." Audrey's tone was friendly, but firm. Dakota knew she meant it.

"Come on, Sadie. We know when we're not welcome," said Dakota in a mock pouting voice. The big dog followed him eagerly down the path to the dock while Patches ran circles around them.

"So what *is* up with you and Tommy?" Audrey asked as soon as Dakota was out of earshot.

Audrey and Erin had the deck to themselves. Mr. and Mrs. Conroy were playing tennis and Mr. Harris was writing, so the girls talked while they watched Dakota trying to encourage Sadie to jump off the dock. He tried everything he could think of, but nothing worked. The big brown dog loved the water and she flew into the lake from shore, but she would not jump from the dock. For some reason the leap was intimidating to her. The girls laughed as Dakota cannonballed off the dock time after time in an effort to coerce the dog to follow him. Patches couldn't make up her mind if she wanted to be in the middle of the action on the dock or cuddled up next to one of the girls on the deck, so she trotted up and down the path between the water and the house.

"So come on now, what *is* up with you and Tommy?" Audrey asked again. "You like him, don't you? I think you two make a cute couple."

"Yes, I like him," admitted Erin readily. She was more than ready to talk about her confusing emotions. "But it's not that simple. Have you seen the way he and Heather act around each other? I'm sure there's something going on between them, but I don't know what. And I can't just ask him." Erin sounded frustrated. "He's so nice to Heather and then he turns around and he's just as nice to me. I don't understand it," Erin added, sounding even more frustrated and confused.

"He's a nice guy. He's nice to everybody – and so is Heather," Audrey said. "But I do know what you mean. I noticed it, too. I'll find out what's going on. We can get Cody to ask Tommy if he has a girlfriend or else I'll just ask Heather." When Audrey saw the panic-stricken look on her friend's face, she quickly added, "Don't worry – I'll be tactful. Too bad we couldn't talk Tommy into coming to the party tonight."

"I don't think he'd have a very good time there, Audrey. You might be used to it, but it can be pretty intimidating to be around rich people," Erin explained.

"They're just like everybody else," Audrey insisted.

"That's exactly what I mean," Erin responded. "You don't even notice it."

"What are you wearing to the party?" Audrey redirected the conversation to one of her favorite topics. "I have that sleeveless blue dress with the matching sweater. I never thought I'd need a sweater on the Fourth of July, but it's been cold at night."

"Think I can just wear jeans and a sweatshirt?" Erin asked, dreading the ordeal of finding something in her limited wardrobe that would be suitable for a party at the snooty rich kids' house.

"Mom and I will help you," Audrey offered kindly. Erin knew she would look great when the Conroy women were done with her, and the thought helped take the edge off her apprehension about the party.

The girl talk came to an end when Audrey's parents returned from playing tennis. Mr. Conroy had won the match and was thoroughly enjoying his victory. The good-natured banter between husband and wife quickly drew the rest of the household into the living room. Dakota and Sadie returned from the lake, soaking wet and cold, and even Mr. Harris tore himself away from his writing. Mrs. Conroy contested some critical points her husband claimed to have won in their tennis match, but she withdrew her complaints when he promised to take her to the Clifton House for brunch in the morning. She always got what she wanted - well, almost always anyway.

Everybody crashed for a few hours of quiet before the party. Audrey's parents were looking forward to seeing the Perrys again, but Mr. Harris declined, saying he was not much of a party-goer. He said he would be perfectly content to stay home with the dogs and watch the fireworks from their dock. Erin wished she could stay home with her father.

Chapter 12

Fourth of July – The Party

The Perry's massive lawn looked like a scene out of a movie, lit with tiki torches and Japanese lanterns. Huge tables were set with red and blue tablecloths and white china, and servers in white jackets carried plates of food and drinks everywhere. There was a barbecue station at one end of the covered patio with heaping platters of ribs and chicken and all the side dishes you could imagine. On the other end of the patio was a dessert station overflowing with buckets of ice cream sitting in bins of ice surrounded by bowls of fruit and candy toppings. A rock and roll band with a dynamite sound system separated the barbecue from the ice cream station. There was even an ice sculpture of a dog that looked just like one of Mr. Perry's American Staffordshire Terriers.

Young people were everywhere – at the tables, filling bowls and cones with ice cream, playing volleyball and Frisbee, and sitting on boats moored at the expansive dock. A few adventurous boys were swimming in spite of the cool evening air.

It was a lot to take in. Erin and Dakota, unused to such lavish displays, stood wide-eyed at the top of the lawn leading down to the water, but Audrey's family was right at home. Mr.

and Mrs. Conroy were greeted like old friends by the twins' parents, who quickly ushered them off to a table for adults on the sidelines of all the activity. Daniel greeted his teen guests in a much more casual manner, but he seemed genuinely pleased to see them – and he seemed especially pleased to see Audrey.

"Come on, I'll show you around," he said to all three of them, but he gestured directly at Audrey to follow him. "Most of the food is on the patio by the band, but there are soda stations and snacks everywhere. The ice cream is really good," he said with a smile just for Audrey. "Most of the kids here are from our school in DC. We're taking the boats out later to watch the fireworks from the water – it's really cool."

Erin was grateful that Audrey and her mother had helped her decide what to wear because at least she didn't feel self-conscious about her clothes. She had insisted on wearing jeans but the Conroy women had made Erin look more sophisticated than she could ever have managed on her own. Audrey lent her a pink silk button-down shirt and Mrs. Conroy had dressed up the outfit with a belt, a scarf and some costume jewelry. Thanks to Mrs. Conroy's magic with styling gel, Erin's short blond hair had a little flip at the end, and even though her low-heeled sandals were a bit tight, she felt pretty comfortable and confident about how she looked. It was a good thing, because the socializing part of the evening was going to be challenging for her. She always marveled at how self-assured Audrey and

Dakota seemed to be in this kind of situation. She was glad she wasn't alone at this party.

"Can we say hi to the dogs?" Erin asked Daniel, wondering where she got the nerve to ask her host for something like that.

Daniel looked a little surprised at her request, but he gave her a positive response. "Sure, but we can't stay long 'cause I have to get back to the party."

When they rounded the corner of the house on the way to the kennels, they had to thread their way through a sea of expensive looking tents pitched on the side lawn. "Most of our friends live too far away to drive home after the party, so we make our own tent village," Daniel explained. "It's become kind of a Fourth of July tradition – it's awesome. We'll probably stay up all night." The last sentence was delivered with another smile solely for Audrey's benefit.

The tents were not like any tents Erin had ever seen. She peeked into several of the open flaps as they made their way to the kennels and was amazed at what she saw. Most of the huge tents were divided into chambers, like little rooms, and there were TV's and stereos, and some even had beds on raised platforms. She actually saw a few port-o-johns in a couple of the tents. It certainly changed her idea about camping. Even Audrey said she could camp like that.

The dogs hurried to sit at attention in the front of their cages as soon as they heard the kennel door open, eagerly awaiting anything they might get from their visitors.   Erin remembered she wasn't supposed to pet them, but it was hard for her to resist. As if to remind her that these dogs were show dogs, the middle-aged man in riding boots stepped out of one of the cages with a box of grooming tools. He nodded curtly, but politely, in the general direction of the teens before disappearing into a little room at the far end of the kennel. Erin recognized him from the day she and Audrey had first met the twins with the dogs in the yard. She assumed the man was the trainer or groomer or dog keeper, and that he probably lived in the little room at the end of the building.

"These really are beautiful dogs," Audrey said. It was obvious she was also trying not to pet them because she had her hands folded in front of her. Erin walked purposely to the far end of the kennel and then returned at a slower pace, looking intently into each individual cage.

"Where's Harry?" she asked with noticeable concern and disappointment in her voice.

"Who?" asked Daniel in response to Erin's question. "Oh yeah - the dog with the lightning bolt on his forehead. We sold him. He wasn't much of a show dog and it turns out he was a real sissy. My Dad has pretty high expectations for these guys. We get rid of them if they can't cut it. They're working dogs, not pets."

"I hope he found a good home," Erin said. "Did you sell him to somebody around here?" she asked.

"I don't know where he is," Daniel stated, obviously uninterested in the dog's fate. "Let's get back to the party. You guys should get something to eat before the fireworks start."

"I'm ready for that – the food looked great," said Dakota, heading for the door with Daniel.

Erin stayed back a few steps to whisper to Audrey, "Don't you dare leave me alone tonight!"

It turned out Erin had a pretty good time. The band was great, the food was great, the fireworks were great, and she actually met some girls she felt comfortable talking to. Erin and Audrey politely sampled the barbecue and side dishes, but they had a hard time stopping Dakota from heaping his plate. He made so many return trips to the buffet that he was on a first name basis with all of the cooks by the end of the evening.

The three of them sat down to eat at one of the tables by the water where they could see their dock across the lake. Audrey said it was a good thing there were so many trees blocking the view because she was sure the Perrys would not appreciate looking at the dilapidated old house from their pristine mansion. Much to the teens' surprise, they saw the two grumpy fishermen slowly circling in the same spot in front of the lake house where they always fished, but they weren't fishing this time. They were just hunched over, watching all the other boats on the lake. None of the other boats got too close to them, probably because the two men looked so grumpy, even from a distance.   It was hard to believe those men were out there to watch the fireworks.

As usual at any party, Audrey was like a magnet, and the seats around her quickly filled up with the twins' friends.   Erin sat quietly and watched as her friend and her brother became the center of attention at a table full of strangers, making it look like the most natural thing in the world.   Dakota, of course, always managed to bring the conversation around to history, but his passion for the subject made it seem exciting to whoever was listening – at least in the beginning.

Audrey, on the other hand, was simply a social butterfly - she loved to talk and she felt comfortable in any situation and she obviously made other people feel comfortable, because they enjoyed being around her.   Erin knew for a fact that Audrey was not aware of how attractive she was, even though she was almost always the prettiest girl wherever they went.   The twins' sophisticated friends, both male and female, were drawn to Audrey, who loved the attention.   Erin talked to some of the more quiet girls and was surprised at how nice they were.   It made her rethink her previous thoughts about snooty rich kids. They weren't all like the twins.   Even though she had a good time, Erin still thought it would have been more fun to spend the Fourth of July with Tommy.   She couldn't stop thinking about that boy.

The party gravitated to the water as the sun set.   Half of the group piled into boats to watch the fireworks and the rest lined the shore to watch the lake fill up with brightly lit boats. It was pretty to watch the boats circling leisurely as it got darker out, waiting for the show to begin. Daniel navigated a huge boat up to the shore next to where Audrey and Erin were standing and waved to them.

"Come on – we can squeeze two more in here," he invited both of them, but again the offer was made directly to Audrey.

"It looks pretty crowded to me," Audrey answered, laughing. "We're fine here, but thanks anyway."

Daniel tried again, "Are you sure? The fireworks should start any minute. It's gonna be a great show and it's really cool to watch from the water."

Audrey waved him off, shaking her head, and told him she wanted take pictures from the shore. Daniel gunned the engine and the boat roared off so quickly a couple of passengers in the back almost went flying into the lake amid peals of laughter.

"Look – there's Dad out on our dock with the dogs!" Dakota waved across the lake, but his father didn't see him. They could make out Sadie sprawled contentedly on the dock by Mr. Harris while Patches paced back and forth nervously.

"She's afraid of fireworks," Audrey explained. There had been isolated rockets going off around the lake for the past hour and the noise had obviously been enough to make Patches nervous. "Aww, look what your Dad's doing. He's so nice."

They watched as Mr. Harris placed a chair right next to him and sat Patches down in it, petting her the whole time. The little dog sat and stared up at the man, and it looked like they were talking to each other. The girls tried to get his attention, but soon it was too dark to see across the lake.

Daniel was right about the fireworks. They were surprisingly good for such a small community. The band played *The Star Spangled Banner* during the show and at times the music and the fireworks seemed synchronized, which was pretty cool. The 'ooohs' and 'aahs' carried across the water from spectators on land and on boats in the middle of the lake. After the fireworks, the band brought the teenage guests back to the present with the new Muse tune from the *Twilight* series.

The ice cream station by the band became a busy place when everybody came off the water. Most of the tables on the patio had been cleared away to make a dance floor which quickly filled with kids eating ice cream while they looked around for dance partners. The band was good.

"Watch out, Audrey," Erin warned. "Daniel will be over here any minute asking you to dance."

Sure enough, as soon as their host had unloaded his passengers and moored his boat, he began scanning the scene on the lawn. Once he spotted Audrey sitting with Erin and Dakota, he started walking purposefully in their direction.

"Come on, Cody," Audrey said swiftly, "save me from him. I don't think I'm up for any more of Mr. Daniel at the moment.   Besides," she added with a smile, "I don't think you and I have ever danced together."

Dakota hesitated just long enough for his sister to notice. *Maybe there is something between those two*, thought Erin. The thought made her feel awkward for some reason and she realized her brother probably felt awkward, too.

"Go on," she encouraged him.   "If you don't dance with Audrey, Daniel will - and so will every other guy here who gets up the nerve to ask her."

"I know," answered Dakota, smiling, "and I bet they're all better dancers than me."   He paused, then stood up and held out his hand.   "Alright, come on Audrey, let's get it over with.   I guess I can handle this."

"What a gentleman," said Audrey facetiously, but she was smiling.

Daniel clearly saw Audrey head to the dance floor with Dakota, but nonetheless he continued walking directly towards the spot where Audrey had been sitting.   Erin was caught totally off guard when the boy stopped in front of her and asked her to dance.   If she had suspected in any way that this was going to happen, she would have had a polite response ready, but she was completely surprised, and at a loss for words.

"Come on, it's a great band," said Daniel, holding out his hand to Erin, who froze for a minute, feeling incredibly awkward. "Come on," he said again.   "It'll be fun."   He was actually being nice.

Erin nodded, coming out of her stupor, and stood up to take his hand without saying a word. Audrey and Dakota did a double take when Erin appeared on the dance floor with Daniel. Once she got over her nervousness, which took a little while, Erin had a blast. They all did.

Chapter 13

Fourth of July – The Day after the Party

The rain came straight down all morning and continued all through the afternoon on the day after the party. It was a welcome excuse to stay in and do nothing, and that's pretty much what the Harris family did. Of course, Mrs. Conroy insisted on brunch at the Clifton House before heading home and of course she coerced her husband and daughter to accompany her. As they headed out, Audrey looked enviously at Erin curled up on the couch with the dogs in front of the TV, but she didn't complain. Her parents were leaving after brunch and she wanted to spend time with them. Besides, she liked the Clifton House.

Mrs. Conroy had been impressed with the Perry's party and she kept the conversation centered on them and their magnificent house throughout their gourmet brunch. She made the same comment about the huge trees blocking their rental house that her daughter had made the night before.

"I'm sure the Perrys would be outraged if they had to look at that dilapidated old house across the lake. It would simply ruin their view. I don't understand how someone can let a house go like that. Thank goodness for those trees. Too bad – it could be a beautiful home" Mrs. Conroy declared as she sampled her Mediterranean omelet. "This food is exquisite," she added.

"And it's one of the biggest lots on the lake," added her husband. "It's probably worth a small fortune."

"I'm glad the owner hasn't sold it, otherwise we wouldn't be here," Audrey chimed in. "This is the best summer I can remember. Thank you both."

"You're very welcome, dear," Mrs. Conroy smiled at her daughter. "Now eat some of that gorgeous waffle." Audrey had a Belgian waffle smothered in fresh blueberries that was almost too pretty to eat.

"The best summer ever, hmmm - could that have something to do with Dakota?" mused her father.

"Or one of the Perry twins?" her mother added.

Audrey blushed and started to eat her breakfast without answering either one of her parents' questions. They didn't ask again.

"Daniel only danced with me so he could interrogate me about you!" Erin insisted when Audrey teased her about the night before.

The girls were playing Liar's Dice with Dakota at the dining room table. The summer rain had not let up and the gentle rhythm of steady drops could be heard through the open windows. Audrey's parents had left after brunch and Mr. Harris had settled back into the master bedroom to write.

"He did pay a lot of attention to you last night, Audrey," Dakota surprised both girls with his comment. He rarely talked about stuff like that and the girls always thought he didn't notice or just didn't care.

"I don't think I got any special treatment," Audrey defended herself. "He danced with every girl there at least once - he was just being a good host. Besides," she continued, "he's not really my type."

"Let's see," countered Erin, "good-looking, sophisticated, rich – nope, not your type at all."

All three of them laughed at Erin's remark and agreed it had been a great party.

"I wonder if Tommy and Heather had a good time up on the rocks," Erin said, trying to sound nonchalant. Before anyone could comment on her remark, Mr. Harris appeared in the living room, much to the surprise of the teens.

"How about a game of Risk?" he asked the group.

"Dad, you tore yourself away from your writing," Erin smiled at her father. "I don't believe it."

"I've stared at that manuscript and that computer screen long enough for one day. It's time for me to join the human race for a while," Mr. Harris said, rubbing his eyes and stretching. "I've actually made some pretty good progress since we've been here. I need to schedule an appointment with my agent soon. But right now, I'm officially off work. Let's play a game."

Dakota dug out the board game and the four of them played for the rest of the afternoon. It was a totally fun way to spend a rainy Sunday afternoon. After Mr. Harris conquered the world in Risk and told stories (which tended to sound like lectures) about world history, he offered to buy pizza for the vanquished players.

"You fly, I'll buy," he told his son. All three teens readily accepted, grinning at his corny remark. Dakota headed out to get the pizza, and the girls took the dogs out for a short walk in the rain. Erin was setting the table when her brother returned.

"Look who I found," exclaimed Dakota as he entered the house with his arms full of pizza boxes. Tommy and Heather were right behind him.

Only Audrey noticed Erin turn beet red as she said a quick hello and busied herself with arranging plates on the table. Everybody else started talking at the same time and Erin was grateful for the distraction – it gave her time to compose herself.

"I set two more plates," she said quietly and actually managed to look at Tommy as she spoke. He gave her one of his great smiles and Erin suddenly realized how glad she was to see him. She had it bad for that boy.

"Thanks," replied Heather. "How was the party? Did you have a good time? Did you like the fireworks?" she asked. "Can I help you with anything?"

"No, it's all done. Let's eat the pizza while it's still hot. I made a salad, too. I hope there's enough. Come on everybody, sit down," Erin prompted, still busying herself with the table. She turned beet red again when Tommy sat down next to her, but she quickly realized it was probably easier for her than having to look across the table right into his face.

"The party was great!" Audrey said, helping herself to a slice of veggie pizza. "And the fireworks, too. Actually, we were all surprised how good they were."

"How was it up on the rocks?" Dakota asked, heaping his plate with slices of pepperoni pizza. "It looks like a cool place. I'd like to go up there sometime."

"It's awesome up there. I'll take you guys sometime," volunteered Heather. "We had a blast last night."

"Except I had to protect Miss Friendly here," Tommy stated, nodding his head in Heather's direction.

"What happened?" chorused Erin, Audrey and Dakota.

"Heather had to be rescued from a passionate admirer," Tommy explained. "Again," he added with emphasis.

"I was just being nice. I didn't want him to kiss me! I don't know why guys always think I'm flirting with them," Heather defended herself.

"You'd think you'd have learned by now," Tommy countered. "This is getting to be a hassle. I'm glad you're my only girl cousin – I don't know if I could handle more than one in the family. "

Erin's mouth dropped open. She met Audrey's eyes and the girls exchanged one of those looks, communicating volumes without saying a word. Heather and Tommy were cousins! A wave of relief swept through Erin's whole body and she felt herself turn beet red again, exhale, relax and smile, all within a split second. No wonder Tommy and Heather were so close.

"Audrey has a similar problem," Dakota explained, "She was like a magnet for every guy at that party last night, but at least I didn't have to defend her honor." He was teasing her.

"Well, I for one am certainly glad to hear that chivalry is alive and well," Mr. Harris smiled at his son and Tommy. "You two boys keep up the good work."

"How's the book coming along, Mr. Harris?" Tommy asked.

"What boy was it, Heather?" asked Audrey curiously. There were two totally different conversations going on at the table.

"Great. I've been doing some research on the Monacan Indians and it's fascinating," Mr. Harris answered Tommy. "I'm going to meet my agent next week and I'm curious to hear his opinion."

"You know the guy that's so good on his skateboard? The one with the wild red hair?" Heather answered Audrey's question with two questions of her own. "He's wild alright," she added smiling.

"The Monacan Indians were native to Dunellon where we live," Dakota explained to Tommy.

Erin sat quietly, content just listening to the two conversations taking place.   She felt great, especially with Tommy sitting next to her - Tommy whose *cousin* was Heather.

Loud voices coming from the water abruptly stopped both conversations.

"What on earth was that?" Heather asked.

"I bet it's those fishermen," Erin answered quickly.   "I'm going out to look."   Sadie and Patches jumped up to follow her and soon the whole group was on the deck peering through the trees, trying to see what was going on.

"There's a light out there," Tommy whispered.   "I think it's that little fishing boat.   See it?" he asked, pointing vaguely towards the lake.   His arm brushed Erin's shoulder when he pointed towards the boat, and she felt a jolt of electricity run through her whole body at his touch.

"Careful, you idiot!" came a gruff voice from the water. "Don't drop it!"

"Why don't you give me a hand instead of just sitting there running your mouth?" came the equally gruff reply.

"What are you doing out there?" asked Mr. Harris in a booming voice.

A loud splash, followed by a string of expletives, echoed up from the water.

"Fishing, and it's none of your business, buddy," shouted one of the men from the boat.

"Let's get out of here," grumbled his companion. "We lost it anyway."

"Dad, don't you think that's weird?" Erin asked her father. "They're out there all the time and they're always so rude."

"Some people are like that, Erin," Tommy said. "Just leave them alone."

"Tommy's right," Mr. Harris said. "Just leave them alone. The lake is a public place and fishing is certainly not against the law – neither is grumpiness."

"Well maybe it should be," Audrey piped up and Heather agreed.

"I wonder who they are. I wonder what they're doing out there," Dakota said.

"Let's go inside," Audrey suggested. "It's wet out here. We can play Liar's Dice – it'll be a blast with so many people."

"Do we have any of that Rocky Road left?" Mr. Harris asked. "I'm ready to fall asleep in front of the TV with a bowl of ice cream. You young folks can play without me." He smiled kindly at his daughter when he said that, but it was too dark outside for Erin to see his expression.

Dakota helped Audrey dish up the ice cream while Erin explained the rules of the dice game to their guests.

Tommy was as good at dice as he was at running and swimming and kayaking and mini-golf, and once again, Audrey's challenges to him made for a lot of laughs. Heather had a hard time understanding the game even though Erin and Dakota coached her as much as they could. The grand finale between Tommy and Audrey had everybody howling. Erin had a sneaking suspicion that Tommy let Audrey win, but nobody else seemed to notice.

Dakota was the first to quit around 10:30, much to the dismay of the others. "I have to get to work early," he explained. "There's a really cool archeology class starting tomorrow at Monticello and I want to see if I can talk someone into letting me tag along." His enthusiasm was obvious.

"If anybody can talk their way into it, you can," laughed Audrey, still excited from winning the game. "You could probably teach the class."

"I don't know about that," responded Dakota modestly. "Have you guys been to Monticello?" he asked Tommy and Heather.

"Oh boy," muttered Erin.

"I haven't been there in years," Tommy answered. "We went there a few times on field trips in school. I would like to see it again."

"Yeah, me too," added Heather. "I remember it was pretty interesting."

"Maybe we can all go next weekend," Dakota said eagerly. "They're having an Old Farm Day. You know, where they dress up and show you how the farm was run in Jefferson's time. There's going to be a cooking demonstration, too - Erin you would like that."

"I guess," his sister replied slowly. "I still can't believe you always want to go there on your days off, Cody. I think you're obsessed with Thomas Jefferson."

"I'll go," Tommy volunteered. "Come on you guys..." His encouragement was directed to the girls in general, but he smiled and looked directly at Erin when he spoke. There was no way she could resist.

"Cool," said Dakota, taking charge. "Let's meet here at 10 o'clock on Saturday morning." Everybody in the group nodded their agreement and decided to call it a night.

"Let's look for Lucy tomorrow morning," Tommy said quietly to Erin on his way out. Her quick genuine smile was the only answer he needed.

Chapter 14

Plans

Erin and Tommy met in the nature preserve on Monday morning, the first of many morning walks together. Even though they didn't see the albino very often, neither of them seemed to mind. They walked and talked for hours at a time and eventually Erin stopped blushing around Tommy. She still felt a little nervous when they were together, but she knew it was just because she had such a crush on him and sometimes she actually enjoyed the feeling. It was kind of exciting.

Erin spent a lot of time talking to Audrey about Tommy. The girls had talked about boys before, but this was the first time Erin had been so serious. They decided Tommy was almost her boyfriend, even though nothing had really happened. Erin kept waiting for that first kiss, but it didn't come - Tommy was always a perfect gentleman. Neither one of the girls thought for a moment that Tommy was seeing anybody else, except for his cousin, and they laughed about how worried Erin had been about Heather.

Most afternoons, the lake house was a gathering place for a random group of teenagers. Erin and Audrey would have a late lunch ready when Dakota got off work, and Mr. Harris usually took a break from his writing to join them. Tommy was there when he wasn't helping his mother, and sometimes Heather showed up if she wasn't working at the Country Store. Even some of Tommy's skateboarding friends showed up on occasion looking for him. Mr. Harris enjoyed the company of the teens and loved to see his children so happy. Sadie and Patches became the spoiled dogs of summer.

Of course, Dakota always started the lunch conversation with a full report about his morning at Monticello. He had indeed managed to convince the director of the archeological field school to let him tag along when he finished mowing the presidential lawns. Dakota was fascinated with the program and couldn't wait to share what he learned with anybody who would listen. He usually had a captive audience at lunch, at least for a brief time while everybody was busy eating, but the energetic group could only listen so long when Dakota talked about things like the ecological and social impacts of switching the main crop at Monticello from tobacco to wheat.

Afternoons were spent kayaking, swimming, playing putt-putt or skateboarding. The group spent hours cannon-balling off the dock into the lake, making up ridiculous contests and dares off the top of their heads. Sadie soon had an entire school of trainers trying to coax her to jump off the dock, but it didn't happen. As much as she loved the water, the dog simply would not be coerced into jumping off a platform when a perfectly good slope down to the lake was available. Patches ran circles around the big brown dog every time they raced back and forth from the dock to the water. Tommy said he'd ask his mother for advice on how to train Sadie to jump. Audrey had her doubts it would ever happen, but this time she kept her thoughts to herself.

Old Farm Day at Monticello was a big hit with everybody. Tommy and Heather showed up as planned and everybody piled into the SUV with Mr. Harris at the wheel. The entire hillside at Monticello was already packed when they arrived and it was like stepping back in time when they got out of the car. There were horse-drawn plows harvesting crops in the fields, blacksmiths, toolmakers, carpenters, cooks, basket weavers, scullery maids and every type of craftsman you could imagine, all in period costumes. Erin sampled most of the cooking, amazed at how good some of it (but not all of it) tasted. Dakota showed his father and Tommy the excavation site of the archeological dig which fascinated him so much. The girls looked at the big hole in the ground for a while, but lost interest in Dakota's detailed description of the dig and wandered off to look at some of the other exhibits.

Erin and Audrey wanted to buy a present for Nora. She was arriving the following day to stay with them for the week while Mr. Harris went off to meet his agent. Both girls adored the housekeeper and were looking forward to her visit, even though they kind of resented the fact that she was being sent as a babysitter. Erin found a handmade basket for Nora and

Audrey bought her a shawl made from llama wool. They were helping Heather find something less expensive for her mother when Audrey spotted the twins.

"Look Erin, there's Daniel. Or is it David?" Audrey asked.

"It's both of them," replied Erin with a total lack of enthusiasm.

"Here they come, whoever they are," quipped Heather.

The twins actually smiled as they approached, which softened Erin's attitude towards them a bit. She hadn't seen them since the party, and she suddenly realized that had only been a week ago. A week with Tommy had changed her perspective on everything. Thinking about Tommy made Erin smile.

"We saw you guys jumping off your dock the other day," said Daniel as a greeting. "We waved, but nobody saw us." He looked directly at Heather, "Hey, weren't you there, too?" Daniel gave her one of his boarding school smiles, turning on the charm.

"Heather, meet Daniel and David. They're twins," Audrey said, grinning. She turned to Daniel, "I'm surprised to see you here. I thought you didn't get involved in local stuff."

"Hi Heather," Daniel and David both spoke at once, like true twins.

"We get credit at school for coming here," Daniel explained.

"Yeah, we have to write a paper on it, but it's the same thing every year," added David. "It's pretty boring."

"I like it," Erin said a bit too aggressively.

"I do, too," piped up Heather. "I think it's interesting." Both twins smiled at her.

"Your party was fun," Audrey changed the subject. "When are you having another one?"

"Hadn't thought about it," said Daniel nonchalantly. "But I doubt we could talk our parents into doing that twice in one summer. My Mom's still complaining about what a mess her house was."

"Why don't you guys have a party?" This time it was David who spoke up.

"I don't know if we could talk my father into that," Erin cautioned.

"At least we wouldn't have to worry about trashing the house," Audrey joked, and Erin had to laugh.

"Sounds like a good idea to me," Heather said brightly. "I love parties." Miss Friendly indeed.

"Erin, let's have a surprise party for Cody! His birthday's in a couple weeks," Audrey was clearly excited about the idea.

"Sure. We can have a surprise archeological dig in the back yard and we can all dress up like Thomas Jefferson. He'll love it," Erin laughed at her own joke.

"Actually, that's not such a bad idea, Erin," said Audrey thoughtfully. "He would love it." She turned to the twins, "We'll let you know if we have a party. Cody's birthday isn't until the 10th of August. That gives us plenty of time."

"Here he comes now," said Erin when she saw her brother approaching with their father and Tommy. "We can talk about it later. When do you guys go back to DC?" she asked the twins.

"We're trying to talk our parents into staying until Labor Day, but I don't like our chances. They want to leave the week before," explained Daniel.

"Hello boys," said Mr. Harris in a friendly tone. "You just missed a very interesting presentation on the history of Monticello." He was teasing his son, but everybody heard the pride in his voice.

The twins greeted Mr. Harris politely, and Dakota introduced Tommy to the boys. Erin was certain she saw a look of superiority on Daniel's face when Tommy shook his hand. Funny, she hadn't seen that condescending look when Heather was introduced. *What a surprise*, she thought, and stopped herself when she realized she was being condescending, too. She had to make an effort to be a little more tolerant than that. After all, the twins had never been mean to her - she just didn't seem to have much in common with them. And of course, she was not at all objective when it came to what anybody thought about Tommy.

Erin was glad when her father said it was time to go, and they all said a quick goodbye to the twins before heading back to the parking lot. There was a lot of housework to do before Nora arrived. When they got back to the car, Dakota and Mr. Harris continued their discussion of the dig at Monticello, and Audrey and Heather talked nonstop about the twins. Erin rolled her eyes at Tommy, letting him know that she found the conversation about the boys silly. He gave her an understanding nod and reached out to take her hand, which sent her into total shock. He held it all the way home, but she felt a warm tingling sensation long after that.

Nora was well-liked by everybody, so her arrival was a big deal. The housekeeper had befriended both Erin and Dakota, each in her own special way. She had spent hours teaching Erin how to cook and just as much time practicing German with Dakota. Nora always had sandwiches or fresh baked cookies and milk waiting when school got out, so Erin and Dakota spent almost as much time in Nora's kitchen as Audrey did. The housekeeper was grateful that her young charge had such good friends and Mr. Harris was grateful for the motherly attention the housekeeper gave his children.

As expected, Nora arrived at the lake house with a ton of home-cooked food. She received a warm welcome from everybody, including the dogs who circled eagerly while the car was unloaded. Mr. Harris had vacated the master bedroom on the main floor to make sure Nora had the best room in the house. She immediately noticed the fresh flowers Erin had put on the dresser and was obviously touched. The housekeeper thanked everybody for making her feel so welcome and almost started crying when the girls gave her the presents they had bought at Monticello.

"Come on outside, Nora. We can sit on the deck and look at the lake. You'll love it," Erin herded everybody out of the house onto the deck. "I made lunch for us. I know it's not like your cooking, but I figured you could take a few minutes to relax before you put on your apron and start spoiling us. We are so looking forward to some good food! If there's one thing I learned this summer, it's that cooking is work. It's fun to make dinner every once in a while, but it's a different story when you have to put dinner on the table every day."

Nora surveyed the table set with a broccoli and cheese quiche, spinach salad and French bread, and her face lit up. "Erin, did you make this yourself? It's beautiful," she said sincerely.

Before Erin could answer, her father spoke. "Erin's been cooking most of the meals since we got here and she's done a great job. I'm proud of her."

"Everybody's been helping," said Erin modestly. "This quiche is a little fancier than usual. We've been having pretty basic stuff and I can't wait to try some different recipes. I feel like we keep eating the same things."

"We can work on that," Nora said encouragingly. "But it looks to me like you're doing quite well. This is delicious."

"When I hear you two talking about food, I almost don't want to leave tomorrow. I know I'm going to miss some good meals," Mr. Harris was serious. "Thank you so much for coming, Nora. I'm sure these guys would be fine on their own, but I feel much better knowing you're here with them."

"My pleasure for sure, Mr. Harris," replied Nora. "It's good for me to get away once in a while. I must say it's been a very quiet summer with all of you out here at the lake."

"We've missed you, Nora," said Audrey sincerely. "I'm glad you came. You'll like it here."

"I'll take you kayaking," Dakota offered spontaneously.

"Nein, Danke," came the prompt reply. "I prefer to enjoy the water from a distance. This deck is just right for me."

As soon as Nora said that, the gruff voices of the fishermen on the lake could be heard below them.

"What on earth is that?" asked Nora with a startled look in her eyes.

"It's our not-so-friendly neighborhood grumpy old fishermen," said Audrey laughing.

Nora responded with a blank look, clearly confused, and Erin explained about the mean old men in the fishing boat.

"I still think they're up to something," Dakota said to nobody in particular.

"Well, please just stay out of their way," his father requested firmly, "especially this week while I'm gone."

With a slightly disgruntled attitude, Dakota promised his father he would leave the fishermen alone. Then he brightened up, "Nora, you have to see Monticello. I can't wait to show you everything."

"That I can do," assured the older woman. "I'm actually looking forward to it. I think we'll have a fun week.   Anything else you kids would like to do?"

"Nora, you have to meet Tommy. Maybe we can invite him over for dinner," Audrey suggested.

"Who is Tommy? Is there something I need to know?" Nora looked intently at Audrey when she asked her questions. Audrey looked at Erin, who immediately started blushing.

"He's somebody we met here at the lake," Audrey explained, trying to take the attention off her friend.

"He's a very polite young man who seems to have taken a shining to my daughter," explained Mr. Harris, much to Erin's surprise.   He looked at his daughter affectionately and continued, "It also appears that she has taken a shining to said young man. He's very nice, Nora – I am sure you'll approve of him when you meet him, which will probably happen very soon."

Erin looked wide-eyed at her father. She couldn't believe he had picked up on the whole Tommy thing, especially since she had just barely figured out what was happening herself. Obviously, her father had a better idea of what was going on with his children than they realized. After her initial shock, Erin realized how kind it was of him to approach the subject the way he did.   He was just letting his daughter know that he understood, and more importantly, that he approved, without embarrassing her. She gave her father an affectionate smile.

"I guess there are no secrets in this house," said Erin smiling. "Nora, he's a really nice guy," she added, a glowing smile spreading across her face as she spoke. Audrey and Dakota grinned at Erin, then at each other, and assured Nora they approved of Tommy, too.

Chapter 15

Everybody Loves Nora

Nora's visit was action packed and the week flew by. She spoiled the teens thoroughly and enjoyed every minute of it as much as the kids did. Monday morning after Dakota left for work and Mr. Harris headed off to Dunellon to meet his agent, the girls gave Nora a guided tour of the area, which turned into a real girls' day out with lunch and antiquing followed by a gourmet grocery store run. The meal planning and grocery shopping were the highlight of the day for Erin and Nora, but they gladly went to the antique stores because they knew how much Audrey enjoyed shopping. Nora rolled her eyes affectionately every time her young charge discovered another treasure, but Audrey did a good job of keeping her spending to a minimum. Erin loved watching the interaction between the two of them, even if it did make her miss her mother.

Nora and the girls planned most of the meals for the week on that first day out, focusing on who would be invited to eat with them - which really just meant Tommy, and maybe Heather. Erin was able to talk Audrey out of inviting the twins, even though Nora's ears picked up every time she heard Audrey mention a boy's name. It was a nice change for the girls to have a woman around and they both gravitated to the housekeeper. Mr. Harris had been doing a great job taking care of the kids at the lake house, but there was no substitute for Nora's grandmotherly affection.

On Tuesday, Nora visited Monticello with Dakota and it was hard to say who enjoyed it more. Dakota loved giving tours of the historical grounds and the housekeeper loved the boy's enthusiasm. Without a doubt, the highlight of the day was the tour of Jefferson's kitchen, where Nora's love of cooking and Dakota's passion for archeology came together.

The boy showed his visitor the vegetable gardens from Jefferson's days, pottery shards and old tools, and explained the importance of the bones found in the ancient trash piles behind the kitchen. Together, all these pieces helped paint a picture of what they ate and how they cooked in Monticello over 100 years ago. Nora was impressed. She was proud of Dakota.

The excited archeologist-to-be continued his historical monologue when they got back to the house, oblivious to the amused glances exchanged by Nora and the girls over lunch. They were all used to it, but they were starting to worry they would be hearing about Thomas Jefferson and the history of Central Virginia until dinner – or maybe even longer. Audrey saved the day by asking Dakota to go kayaking with her. The hot weather had returned as soon as the rain stopped after the Fourth of July, and being in or on the water every day was the best way to handle the heat.

Nora and Erin sat quietly on the deck and simply enjoyed each other's company while they watched the two colorful boats glide across the water. The housekeeper took advantage of the opportunity to talk to Erin about "this boy Tommy," smiling patiently when Erin blushed and struggled for words. Nora listened when Erin talked about how nice Tommy was and confessed how nervous she was around him.

"That's perfectly normal," Nora assured her. "I'm looking forward to meeting him. Why don't you invite Tommy and his cousin for dinner tomorrow night? I'm making pot roast – your favorite."

Dakota's booming voice interrupted the girl talk before Erin could answer. He and Audrey were putting the boats away and he wanted Sadie to practice jumping off the dock, probably to show off in front of Nora. As soon as Dakota called Sadie, the eager dog tore down to the dock with Patches doing her circle dance around her, and it looked like this time she just might go flying off the dock into the water. Everybody burst out laughing when Sadie stopped dead in her tracks on the dock, right at Dakota's side, wagging her tail and looking as happy as could be. Next to them, Patches did her little swimming dance in ankle deep water. It was hysterical.

The little group spent the rest of the afternoon hanging out, talking and swimming, and playing with the dogs. Nora made a huge pot of fettuccini Alfredo and a Caesar salad which they enjoyed on the deck, and they stayed outside long after it got dark. It finally cooled off a little by the time the stars came out and it was late before any of them went to bed. They all agreed it had been a perfect day.

Nora and Audrey joined Erin the next morning for her walk in the nature preserve. There was no sign of Lucy, but the woods were beautiful and the housekeeper loved it. Audrey must have taken about a thousand pictures - she was certainly putting her camera to good use. They walked all the way through the preserve to the neighborhood where Tommy lived and Audrey kept going, leading the way right up to his little house. Erin objected half-heartedly, but she was actually glad to see Mrs. Jackson working in the yard when they walked by. Tommy's mother greeted them warmly and she really hit it off with Nora. Before Erin knew what was happening, Nora had invited Mrs. Jackson to dinner that evening with Tommy and Heather.

"Tommy's at the vet with a new dog we inherited," Mrs. Jackson explained. "This poor fellow just wandered up to the house yesterday in really bad shape and almost collapsed on our doorstep. The vet said it looked like he had been in a bad fight - turns out he had a broken leg and the vet had to stitch him up in several places, too. They put him on antibiotics because some of the wounds looked like they might be infected. He seems to be doing much better today, but the vet wanted to see him again just to make sure he was alright, so Tommy volunteered to take him this morning."

"Well that dog knew exactly where to come to get the care he needs," Erin said laughing. She hadn't seen Tommy in two days and she was relieved to hear there was a reason for it. "That dog is either incredibly smart or just plain lucky." She turned to Nora and explained, "You can't see it from here, but out back Tommy and his mother have a huge kennel and eight - make that nine - dogs that they've rescued over the years." To Mrs. Jackson, she said, "I can't believe you took in another stray. You guys are so kind. I can't wait to meet him. What kind of dog is he?"

"Tommy can give you a full report tonight, dear," Mrs. Jackson explained to the girl. "He and Heather are really looking forward to this dinner, and so am I, now that I'm invited, too. What a nice surprise. Can we bring anything? Dessert?"

"I think we're all set, but thank you for asking," Nora replied. "I have a lot of help with these girls here. They don't know it yet, but they're making strawberry pie for dessert." Nora smiled at the surprised looks on the girls' faces. "As a matter of fact, we should probably be going. They have a lot of work to do."

"Well, Nora, it was nice meeting you. Thank you again for the invitation," Mrs. Jackson said. "We'll see you this evening."

The whole way home, Erin talked about Tommy and his mother. It was Audrey's turn to exchange amused looks with Nora.

The dinner was awesome. As had been expected, Nora wholeheartedly approved of Tommy and called him "a very polite young man." It certainly didn't hurt his image any that he arrived with a bouquet of flowers for Nora and an incredible smile for Erin. Heather brought Nora a box of chocolates from a local specialty shop, so needless to say, the housekeeper thoroughly enjoyed her guests.

After dinner and a wonderful strawberry pie with whipped cream, they walked down to sit on the dock with their feet dangling in the water. It was cool and relaxing and the lake was like an inviting dream at the end of the hot summer day, so it wasn't long before the young people ended up swimming. Of course, the boys were the first to cannonball off the dock, but it was only a matter of minutes before the girls followed. It was simply irresistible. Nora and Mrs. Jackson watched the teens and the dogs and reminisced about their own summer nights as young girls.

Tommy worked his dog magic on Sadie and she almost, *almost*, jumped from the dock. Erin thought it was amazing, but then she pretty much thought everything about Tommy was amazing.

It was late when they finally left the cool water and the dock and made their way back up to the house. Tommy headed for the dungeon with Dakota to borrow some dry clothes while the girls headed upstairs to change. Audrey was rummaging around in her closet for just the right shorts and tee shirt when she heard a scratching sound outside her window. *Oh, those boys think they are so funny*, she thought as she wandered over to her balcony to check out the noise, certain she would find Dakota climbing up the side of the house to the little balcony outside her room.

It took a minute for Audrey's eyes to adjust to the dark as she stepped out onto the small deck, but her ears had no problem finding the source of the noise. A scuttling, scratching sound came from the tree directly in front of her. Still expecting to see the boys, Audrey walked forward with her hands on her hips and peered defiantly into the darkness surrounding the tree. A pair of eyes peered right back at her. Startled, the girl took a step away from the tree, and as her eyes continued to adjust to the dark, she saw another pair of eyes set in a bandit face looking directly at her. Raccoons! A smile spread across Audrey's face as she surveyed the tree and discovered three young raccoons nestled in forks in the branches, watching her with curious expressions.

Audrey backed away as quietly as possible, trying not to startle the young raccoons. She wanted Erin and Heather to see this. She was almost back in her room when she spotted a larger raccoon, probably the mother, perched on a much higher branch watching Audrey watch her babies. It was too cute. Audrey finally made it back into the house and ran to the opposite end of the hall to get the other girls. The three of them tiptoed cautiously back down the hall and snuck out onto Audrey's little deck as quietly as possible, not really expecting the visitors to still be there.

"Aaahhhhh," chorused Erin and Heather at the same time when they spotted the raccoons.

"They're adorable," Erin said with awe in her voice. "I'm going to get Nora and Mrs. Jackson and the boys," she said, tiptoeing off the balcony into the house. Audrey ran back in to get her camera and reappeared in less than a minute.

Heather and Audrey watched the baby raccoons intently for what seemed like an hour before Erin appeared with the others. After several choruses of "ooohhhs" and "aaahhs," Nora spoke up.

"OK, those guys are incredibly cute, no doubt about it, but I don't trust this rickety old deck. I'm going back inside," the housekeeper said seriously.

"I have to agree with you," Mrs. Jackson echoed emphatically. "Besides, it's late and we really should go. I'm glad we got to see these little rascals, though. Tommy, Heather, are you ready?" Her question was really a statement.

Mrs. Jackson had to prompt Heather and Tommy again to get them to move. They didn't want to leave. One by one, everybody on the deck had one last look at the little bandits in the tree and marched back into the house through Audrey's room before saying goodnight.

Chapter 16

A Hunch

Nora and the girls cornered Mr. Harris the minute he walked in the door on Friday morning to tell him about their plans to surprise Dakota on his birthday, August 10th. Mr. Harris loved the idea and promised to help any way he could, so the conspirators managed to outline their plans as much as possible before the unsuspecting victim came home from work. Mrs. Jackson and Heather had already promised to help with the food and Tommy had offered to be in charge of distracting Dakota in order to make sure the birthday boy arrived in the right place at the right time. The adults gave the girls some tips on how to pull off the surprise and what foods would be easy to prepare for a group of people. Nora was sorry she wouldn't be there to help, especially since she would love to see the look on Dakota's face, but she knew the party would be a success.

Nora's last night was fun. They all helped her cook up a storm even though Mr. Harris offered to take everybody out for dinner. He wanted to show his appreciation to Nora, but she resisted adamantly, saying it was her pleasure to spend a week with the teens. Needless to say, nobody complained about one last home-cooked meal. Nora's lasagna, spinach salad and garlic bread disappeared quickly, in spite of the fact that it was almost too hot outside to eat.

The little group sat on the deck for a long time after dinner waiting for it to cool off, but it never did. Mr. Harris had brought a cherry cheesecake from their favorite Dunellon bakery to celebrate the good review his agent had given his manuscript. He was especially proud of the fact that the original idea for the book had come from his children, and he wanted them to know how much their contribution meant to him.

The past winter, shortly after Audrey's family moved to Dunellon, the three teenagers had shocked the entire community when they discovered previously unknown facts about the history of their hometown. They had foiled a ruthless businessman's plot to exploit the tribal Indians in Dunellon, and then encouraged the man to donate funds to build a community center.   This adventure had inspired Mr. Harris to write about the history of Dunellon. They were all pretty excited about it.

Nora beamed when the teens were praised, looking especially proud of Audrey. It was obvious the housekeeper adored her, and Nora got more and more sentimental as the evening wore on.

"Well, I'll be glad when the summer's over and all of you come back home," she said in an emotional tone. "But I certainly want you to have fun and enjoy your summer," she added. "I can see why you like it here. I had a great time this week."

"We did, too, Nora," Audrey answered promptly. "It was so good to see you. I've really missed you."

"And thank you for all the fantastic meals and the cooking lessons," added Erin affectionately. "It was great to try some new recipes and have some real help with kitchen duty. Who knows, with your help I might actually learn to cook one day."

Erin's last statement was met with a chorus of voices insisting she was already a good cook. The praise made her feel uncomfortable and she was glad they were sitting outside in the dark so no one could see her blush.

"Auf Wiedersehen und vielen Dank," said Dakota affectionately. "Thanks for practicing German with me. I know I'm going to need a lot of help next year in school."

"Half the summer is already gone," said Mr. Harris. "I can't believe it. We'll be back at home before you know it. Thank you so much for coming, Nora. It was greatly appreciated by all." With that, he stood up and gave the housekeeper a big hug and headed off to bed. The others followed shortly.

There was a noticeable sense of urgency in the air after Nora left. Maybe, as Mr. Harris had said, it was because half the summer was gone and the little group would be back in Dunellon before they knew it. Everybody had enjoyed the lake house from the start, but now they made a conscious effort to make every day count - each of them felt a keen awareness that their days of summer were numbered.

Audrey started to join Erin on her morning walks in the nature preserve more often, sharing a little bit of magic whenever they saw Lucy. The girls spent hours trying to get some good photos of the albino, but the shy creature was elusive and it was hard to get close enough for a really good shot. Tommy was often with them on their walks and he was almost always at the lake house after lunch. When Dakota was there, they kayaked and swam and cannonballed off the dock and played games and went miniature golfing and ordered pizza. The bonds of friendship strengthened between the teens with every passing day.

The relationship between Erin and Tommy intensified, adding to the sense of urgency felt by the residents of the lake house. Everybody speculated about what was going to happen when they were separated at the end of the summer. Mr. Harris was concerned for his daughter – not because he didn't approve of Tommy, but because he knew the separation would be painful for her. It was hard for him to think about his little girl dealing with such a difficult adult situation. He decided it was time to meet the boy's mother.

Mrs. Jackson gratefully accepted Mr. Harris's dinner invitation. She had her own concerns about the relationship between the two young people and was thankful for the opportunity to meet Erin's father. Tommy's mother knew

Dakota and Audrey, of course, and Nora's dinner at the lake house had given her some insight into Erin's family, but it wasn't the same as meeting a parent.

"I'm glad your Dad invited my Mom for dinner tonight," Tommy said to Erin. The two of them were sitting on the rocks overlooking the lake, holding hands and talking. "It's about time they met because it's the only way we'll be able to see each other after summer's over." He squeezed her hand and Erin felt that surge of emotion which always overcame her when she was around Tommy. She was actually getting used to it and sometimes she even enjoyed the emotional rollercoaster. "You're right," said Erin quietly. "There's no way my father would let you visit us in Dunellon without meeting your mother. And I sincerely doubt he'll *ever* let me come back here to see you," she sighed.

"Hey, let's not worry about that now," Tommy reassured her, squeezing her hand again. "We should just enjoy the rest of the summer."

"What the heck is that?" Tommy let go of Erin's hand and jumped up excitedly, pointing down at the lake. It took Erin a minute to see what he was talking about, but then she made out the two grumpy old fishermen in front of their lake house.

"It looks like they're dragging something up out of the water," Erin said slowly, squinting to get a better look. "Can you see what it is?" she asked.

"No, but for some reason I doubt it's a fish," Tommy said flatly.

"Tommy, I know those men are up to something. Dakota thinks so, too. Look at them – that is not the way fishermen behave. Do you believe me now?" Erin was almost pleading with him.

"Actually, yes I do, Erin," Tommy answered sincerely, giving her one of his to-die-for smiles.

"Well how are we going to find out what they're doing? We need a plan," she said as soon as could speak. Sometimes Tommy's smile took her breath away.

"Do you have a camera?" he asked.

"Audrey does. She's always taking pictures," Erin answered.

"Let's go," Tommy took her hand again and they headed down the rocks to the path around the lake. "We need to take turns and watch those guys around the clock. We need to find out what they're up to and we need evidence to prove it - otherwise nobody is going to listen to us." Erin couldn't believe how serious he sounded.

"And I don't want you going near those men. We are only going to watch them from a distance and take pictures. Understand?" He stopped in his tracks and turned to face her while he waited for her reply.

"Déjà vu," said Erin quietly with a grin on her face.

"Erin, please, I'm serious. Promise me."

"OK, OK, I'll stay away," she said reluctantly.

"Promise me, Erin, please." It was obvious he wasn't going to give up.

"I promise," Erin said, "but you have to promise, too."

Tommy also hesitated for quite a while before answering, searching her eyes as if to question her seriousness. "I promise." His words sounded intense.

"What's different now, Tommy?" Erin questioned him pointedly. "Those men have been out there the whole summer and I couldn't convince you there was anything suspicious about them. What made you change your mind now?" There was confusion in Erin's voice.

"That's just it – they've been out there the whole summer. This is not some freaky thing we just saw once or twice. And I really don't believe they're fishing. Something about the way they were moving today looked funny, like they were trying to hide something. Most fishermen can't wait to show everybody what they have in their boat." He squeezed Erin's hand again, "Call it a hunch," he whispered.

Dinner at the lake house that evening was interesting. Mr. Harris and Mrs. Jackson carried on a polite, parent-like conversation, while their children started planning covert operations. It had taken Dakota and Audrey about two seconds to agree with Tommy's plan and they were eager to get started, but they were going to be discreet about it.

Erin impressed everybody with her chicken and vegetables on the grill, and Mrs. Jackson surprised them all with her specialty - homemade blueberry pie. Tommy looked proud of his mother's efforts and he enjoyed the praise both Erin and his mother got from the others. Finally, after dessert on the deck, the teens were able to start outlining their espionage strategy. They hid their intentions under the pretense of looking at the ton of pictures Audrey had taken at the lake house over the summer. They brought Audrey's laptop and camera out onto the deck, really just to make sure the camera was charged, but soon they were all sidetracked looking at the pictures.

"I don't believe it – our first kayaking lesson!" Erin laughed at a really awkward picture of herself in a kayak. "It seems like years ago..."

"Look at that one, Erin," Audrey said, pointing. "You almost capsized trying to get that stupid leaf out of the water, remember?"

It was definitely cool to see their summer in pictures. Of course, Erin was more interested in the later ones because there were several pictures of Tommy. Audrey noticed her friend's preoccupation and tried to distract her.

"Look, Erin," she said. "There's a shot of Lucy. It's not that good, but we can edit it. That's from the morning she was in our yard, remember? We need to get some good pictures of her before the summer's over."

"Let's take the camera with us on our walk tomorrow morning," Erin said loudly enough for her father and Mrs. Jackson to hear. She gave Audrey and the boys an exaggerated wink as if to say, *so we can take pictures of the grumpy old fishermen.* It didn't take long for the others to crack up laughing at her corny attempt at spy humor.

They arranged a schedule of sorts to make sure the camera was charged at all times, and that at least one of them would be watching the lake, especially during daylight hours. Even though they seriously doubted the fishermen would try anything over the weekend because of all the people on the water, they agreed they should keep an eye on them just in case. They weren't too sure how to manage the nights, but they agreed it was important to keep an eye on the fishermen whenever possible.

The spies had a plan in place by the time Mrs. Jackson told Tommy she was ready to leave, even though they weren't too sure what they were looking for. They did agree that the grumpy fishermen were suspicious, but they couldn't really explain why. And they agreed that there was something to Tommy's hunch, but they couldn't explain that either. One thing Audrey and Dakota *could* explain was the huge smile on Erin's face when Tommy said he'd meet her in the nature preserve in the morning.

Chapter 17

Harry

The early morning sun held the promise of another incredibly hot day. Tommy met the girls in the nature preserve at the spot where he had first met Erin, and where they often saw Lucy. Erin was hoping to see the albino on their walk, but Audrey was convinced there would be no sign of her because they didn't have the camera with them. Dakota had it with him on his first shift of spy duty.

"It's like a law of nature," Audrey explained with a wry smile on her face. "I call it the umbrella principle. If you have an umbrella with you, it won't rain, but if you don't bring your umbrella, it pours." She looked to her companions for confirmation before continuing, but she continued talking even when she didn't get any support for her theory. "And whenever I don't have my camera with me, I see some incredible photo ops."

"So what you are saying is, whoever has spy duty should *not* have the camera if they want to get a shot of the grumpy old fishermen in action? That if they have a camera, nothing will happen and if they don't have a camera, something will happen for sure?" Tommy asked.

He waited for a nod of agreement from Audrey before he finished, "so if we follow this theory to its logical conclusion, it means nobody will ever get a photograph of anything worthwhile, because things worth photographing won't be seen if there is a camera available." Tommy grinned from ear to ear, obviously enjoying himself.

"OK, OK, I give," Audrey conceded good-naturedly. "I should have known better than to put a random thought out there with you around."

Erin smiled up at Tommy, but said nothing. She enjoyed listening to the teasing between her two friends and felt totally comfortable letting them do all the talking. She was in heaven just walking through the woods at Tommy's side. He took her hand in his and gave it an affectionate squeeze and shot her one of his magical smiles before asking Audrey if she had any other theories she'd like to test.

"Not this morning, smart aleck," came the prompt reply. "But just watch – I bet we don't see any sign of Lucy today."

Sure enough, their quiet march through the morning woods was wonderful, but they didn't see the albino or any other deer. When they were almost through to the other side of the preserve, Audrey spoke up, "Tommy, can we see your new dog since we're almost at your house?"

"Yeah, that's a great idea," Erin said. "I have been dying to meet him. And we can thank your mother for the blueberry pie. I had some for breakfast this morning and I bet my tongue's still purple."

"Thanks for the lovely visual on that, Erin," said Audrey laughing, "but that pie really was excellent. Your Mom won't mind if we just drop in, will she?"

"Knowing my mother, she probably already has breakfast waiting for you," Tommy answered. "I told her we were walking together this morning. She likes you guys," he added. "I think she's hoping some of your manners and your smarts will rub off on me."

"Fat chance," quipped Audrey, and they all laughed.

As Tommy predicted, Mrs. Jackson was waiting on the front porch when they turned up the little side street. As they got closer to the house, the unmistakable aroma of baking biscuits filled the air.

"That smells heavenly, Mrs. Jackson," Erin said. "I think I might have to try my hand at baking some time – maybe at Christmas."

"I'll have a talk with your father, dear. Maybe we can arrange for you to visit us over the holidays. I'm sure we can manage something," Mrs. Jackson said warmly. That statement put a huge smile on both Tommy's and Erin's faces. "Now come on in and have a seat. Breakfast will be ready in just a few minutes. I wanted to make sure you were all here before I started the eggs." The woman ushered them in and busied herself in the kitchen.

"Mom, the girls want to meet our new dog," said Tommy. "Do we have time before breakfast?"

"Yes, if you hurry," replied his mother as she busied herself at the stove. "Maybe the girls can help us think of a name for him. Poor thing seems to be doing much better this morning, but he's definitely been looking for you, Tommy."

The teens headed for the back door, promising to be back in a minute for their breakfast. Halfway out the door, Erin stopped so quickly that Audrey ran right into her.

"Harry!" shouted Erin as soon as she saw the dog with the lightning bolt scar on his forehead sitting on the porch. "Audrey, look!" Erin was beside herself. She knelt down and looked at the dog, who had a splint on one of his front legs and cuts and stitches everywhere. She let him sniff her hand and then gently scratched the dog behind his ears.

"I don't believe it," Audrey exclaimed. Her reaction was a bit quieter than Erin's, but no less intense. "That dog belongs to the twins across the lake. They told us they sold him!" There was anger in her voice.

Erin was almost in tears, "Tommy, I'm so glad you found him. See that scar on his forehead? I called him Harry because he has a lightning bolt scar just like Harry Potter. Where did you find him? What did the vet say?" Erin stopped talking for a minute and the look on her face became serious. "What do you think happened?" she asked. "Do you think the twins know about this? Did those boys do this to Harry?"

"The boys or their father," Audrey added intensely.

"Is everything alright?" Mrs. Jackson came out onto the back porch to see what Erin was shouting about, wiping her hands on her apron.

"I don't know, Mom," Tommy said. "The girls know who owns this dog and apparently the owners told them the dog had been sold. They're pretty upset."

"I can't believe anybody would abandon such a sweet creature. We'll call animal control, but for now we might as well talk over breakfast instead of standing on the porch," Mrs. Jackson said logically. "Your food's getting cold inside and it's getting hot out here. Come on in and bring that little feller with you. He can sit in the kitchen while we eat."

Tommy and his mother listened intently while the girls told them everything they remembered about Harry and his owners. The injured dog slept at Erin's feet, enjoying the occasional pets he got from everybody in the kitchen. The more they talked about the situation over breakfast, the more they realized this was a complicated, and potentially criminal, situation.

"We should talk to Dad. He'll know what to do," Erin said in between bites of warm biscuits and fresh strawberry preserves. In spite of their genuine concern for the seriousness of the situation, they all managed to eat. Harry slept through everything, sighing occasionally.

"I'll call my parents, too," Audrey added.

"Good idea," said Mrs. Jackson. "Erin, I would like to talk to your father. I know a lot of people around here who might be able to help us get to the bottom of this. Tommy, why don't you take my car and drive the girls home? And Erin, will you please ask your father to call me? Maybe he and I can get together sometime this afternoon. In the meantime, I'll make sure this poor guy gets some food and I'll change his bandage." She looked affectionately at the sleeping dog. "He'll be fine – I'll see to that, but he still has a long way to go."

The teens thanked Mrs. Jackson for breakfast and each of them gave Harry another pet before heading back to the lake house. Erin was more upset than any of them, probably because she had bonded with Harry the very first time she saw him. The whole way home she just kept shaking her head, muttering to herself. Tommy and Audrey said nothing.

Dakota was glad to see them, eager for some relief from the monotony of spy duty. As if to prove Audrey's camera theory, he had been bored to death all morning. It was a weekend, so there were a lot of people on the lake and there was no way the fisherman could have done anything without being observed by someone else nearby on the water. The grumpy old men had just sat in their boat in the same spot as always and all Dakota had done all morning was watch them. The boy was about to launch into a diatribe about just how boring his spy duty had been when the serious look on his sister's face stopped him.

"What's up, Erin?" he asked with concern. "What happened?" He looked to his two friends for an explanation.

"Remember the dog at the twins' house with the lightning bolt on his forehead?" Audrey jumped in to explain for her friend. "Well, he's the dog that turned up at Tommy's house last week that was so badly injured."

"Are you sure it's the same dog?" Dakota asked. "We only saw him a couple of times."

"I'm sure, Cody," answered Erin firmly, but not unkindly, as she walked past him into the house. "I'm going to get Dad."

"She's pretty upset," said Tommy with concern in his voice. "I think it'll be good for her to talk to your father. My mother wants him to call her so she can help find out what happened. I just wanted to make sure Erin got home OK. Will you tell her I'll come back later?" Tommy got into his car with a worried look on his face and distractedly waved goodbye to Dakota and Audrey as he drove off.

Sitting at Mrs. Jackson's kitchen table that afternoon, Mr. Harris was as level-headed and logical as everybody had expected. The girls had filled him in on the situation earlier and he had immediately agreed to meet with Mrs. Jackson. As was his nature, he stressed the need to proceed with caution. Animal abuse was a serious crime and the legal aspects of the situation concerned him. He was also worried about Erin's reaction to the situation, so he did his best to remain calm for her sake.

When Audrey called her parents, Mr. Harris spent a long time on the phone with them, listening to both Mr. and Mrs. Conroy. They were business people and offered some sound advice and practical suggestions about how to proceed.

Mr. Harris's first conclusion was that there was no real evidence of a crime and no proof the Perrys were guilty of cruelty to animals. A false accusation could be disastrous. On the other hand, the dog had been severely injured and something had to be done about it. That's where Mrs. Jackson came in. She had a lot of experience with Animal Control and apparently knew everybody at Lake Bonita. Well, almost everybody – she didn't know the Perrys.

"There won't be anyone on duty at Animal Control until Monday," she explained, "and I think we should talk to them first. They're actually part of the police department and they'll take a statement from us and start a proper investigation. They're actually pretty good."

"I think it would be a good idea to have a talk with Mr. and Mrs. Perry before we do anything," Mr. Harris suggested. "After all, they might have an explanation for what happened. I doubt it, but they should at least have a chance to explain what happened before we go to the authorities. I think it's the right thing to do." He turned to Audrey, "That was one of the first things your parents suggested, too."

"I guess you're right," said Mrs. Jackson slowly. "Maybe the dog got lost and was injured after that somehow." She sounded skeptical at first, but she continued with more conviction, "Besides, all we have so far is third-hand information from our children." She turned to Tommy and Erin, "Sorry guys," she said with a smile, "but I'm sure you know what I'm getting at."

Tommy and Erin had listened quietly while their parents discussed what to do, and both teens nodded their understanding in response to Mrs. Jackson's comment. They were the only kids present at the Jackson's kitchen table because Audrey and Dakota had volunteered for spy duty. It was especially thoughtful of Dakota after he had been so bored on the morning watch, but he knew how Erin felt about Harry and he knew she wanted to be a part of the meeting with the grown-ups, so he had volunteered again. Besides, Audrey was there to keep him company, and the two of them were going to take the kayaks out so they could spy from the water.

"I'm a little worried about getting the children involved," said Mr. Harris seriously. "If this is a criminal offense there could be repercussions and I wouldn't want their names to be publicized." He looked at Erin and Tommy. "Understand?" It was more of a parental decree than a question.

"I agree," responded Mrs. Jackson before either of the teens had a chance to speak. "I'll make the statement with

Animal Control so that my name will be the only one anybody sees,"

"I guess the first thing to do is call the Perrys," said Mr. Harris slowly. "I don't want to just knock on their door. Do you think I should tell them about Harry or just say I need to discuss a serious matter?" He looked to everyone at the table for an answer.

"I think you should say you want to talk to them about their dogs," Erin replied.

"And let them know it's serious," added Tommy.

"Let's just call them right now," Mrs. Jackson jumped and got the phone book, laid it on the kitchen table, and opened it to find the number she wanted. "Here it is," she said. "Would you like me to call?"

"No, thank you," answered Mr. Harris, picking up the phone. "I'll call them now – no time like the present." As he dialed, he muttered under his breath, "This should be interesting."

Chapter 18

Stormy

The weather after the meeting at Jackson's seemed to reflect the worry and stress about Harry. The hot blue skies above the lake slowly turned grey, then black, and by late afternoon the heavens opened up. Audrey and Dakota barely managed to get back to shore in their kayaks before the rain started, and they were completely soaked by the time they got the boats out of the water. Sadie and Patches greeted them wildly at the door, nervous because of the storm and also because they had been alone all afternoon. Neither one of the dogs wanted to go out in the storm, so Dakota had to coax them back out while Audrey put food in their bowls. Both teens were still in wet clothes when Erin and Mr. Harris returned.

"I'm glad you two are off the water," said Mr. Harris to Audrey and Dakota when he walked into the kitchen. "I was worried about you."

"We got back here before the storm hit, but then we got soaked putting the boats away," Audrey said, shaking her wet hair. "How did it go?" she asked in a concerned voice, looking back and forth to both Erin and her father for an answer.

Father and daughter exchanged glances before Mr. Harris answered. "Mrs. Jackson and I are going to talk to the Perrys tomorrow evening," he explained. "I called this afternoon and Mrs. Perry said her husband was out of town on business, but he would be back tomorrow. She seemed hesitant to schedule a meeting with us on a Sunday afternoon, but I told her it was urgent."

"Did you tell her what it was about?" Dakota asked.

"Sort of," Mr. Harris answered hesitantly. "She immediately asked if it had to do with the twins, so I told her it was about the dogs in order to reassure her. I know your mother would have been worried about you if she had received a phone call like that." A sad smile crossed his face at the mention of his wife. He shook his head and continued speaking thoughtfully, "I got the impression Mrs. Perry doesn't really care much about those dogs."

"I don't think anybody in that family cares about those dogs," said Erin angrily. "Mr. Perry and the twins just like to brag about the prizes the dogs win at their fancy shows. They talk about breeding them all the time, but I doubt they even know their names. The trainer seems to be the only one who spends any time with them."

"I hope the trainer will be there this afternoon," said Mr. Harris thoughtfully. "I should have mentioned that to Mrs. Perry on the phone." He looked pensive for a minute. "At any rate, I'm glad we're meeting with them before going to the authorities. There's probably more to this than I thought. There usually is," he added.

"What's for dinner?" asked Dakota suddenly.   "I'm starved."

"There's a bunch of leftovers from last night," Erin said.

"Do we have any other choices?" Audrey asked.   "You know I don't really like to have the same thing two nights in a row."

"I'll treat you guys to pizza if we get delivery," offered Mr. Harris.   "No way I'm going out again in that weather unless I have to."

"Nobody needs to go out," said Erin seriously.   "There's some of Nora's spaghetti sauce with meatballs in the freezer.   It wouldn't take long to heat up.   How does that sound?"

"Great!" said Audrey.   "Thanks, Erin.   Spaghetti's a perfect dinner for a stormy night and I'll make a salad if you guys want.   You did a great job last night, Erin - it was a very good dinner," she added, complimenting Erin on the meal she had cooked for Tommy and his mother.   "I just would prefer something different tonight.   No offense," Audrey said sheepishly.   She looked a little worried that she might have offended her friend.

"No offense taken," Erin said, smiling at Audrey.   "I think I need some comfort food anyway and spaghetti sounds perfect to me.   I will definitely take you up on your offer to make a salad while I put the water on and heat up the sauce."

Except for the thunder and lightning outside, it was a quiet evening at the lake house.   Everybody enjoyed their dinner even though they couldn't stop talking and worrying about Harry. Mr. Harris found himself repeatedly reminding the teens not to speculate about the Perry family's involvement, even though he found himself just as guilty of jumping to conclusions in his own mind. "We'll have more information tomorrow," he said every time one of the kids brought up the subject. "Let's not make any judgments until we have all the facts." Sometimes he sounded just like a parent.

Before they went to bed, Erin had a chance to ask Audrey if anything had happened on the lake that afternoon, but of course Audrey had nothing to report. It had been a normal busy Saturday afternoon before the storm drove everybody off the water, and she and Dakota had just watched the grumpy old men sit in their boat the whole afternoon until the rain came. Audrey said it would have been incredibly boring if she had been alone, but out in the kayaks with Dakota it had been fun. She suggested they should team up for spy duty from now on, and when Erin volunteered to pair up with Tommy, Audrey burst out laughing, gave her friend a big hug and went to bed.

Erin had wild nightmares that night. Maybe it was the storm or worrying about Harry or talking about kayaking before bed, but something lent a very dark edge to her dreams. She dreamt she was kayaking with her brother on the lake in the middle of winter and ice had formed along the shallow shoreline, making it difficult to paddle. The ice was thin and almost invisible, and before she could even see it she could hear the crunching noises her boat made when it hit the brittle surface.

This should be fun, Erin kept thinking in the dream, but instead she felt a terrible sense of foreboding. Dakota was there, leaning over the side of his boat trying to see something on the bottom of the lake while Erin kept chasing after a leaf frozen in a chunk of ice. Suddenly, the pale winter sky above them darkened and a flock of crows flew so close overhead they could hear the wings flapping. The sound was ominous.

Erin sat up in bed with a shudder, not sure where she was or what was happening, and it took her a moment to wake up enough to grasp that she had been dreaming. The spot in her dream where she had been chasing a frozen leaf was familiar to her. She suddenly realized it was the exact same spot where the grumpy old fishermen always sat. For some reason, Erin knew she needed to remember this. It was important. Then she went back to sleep.

By Sunday morning the storm had not let up, and it even got worse as the day went on. Tommy and his mother were supposed to come over to the lake house at 2:30 so the adults could be at the Perry's by 3:00, but they came over early and everybody had lunch together. (The leftovers finally got eaten.) It just seemed like the right thing to do on a dark and dreary day when they were all thinking about the same thing – Harry. Mrs. Jackson had left the dog sleeping soundly in her kitchen, safe and warm, and she reassured everybody that Harry was making a great recovery. Her main concern now was saving the rest of the Perry's dogs from a similar fate.

Of course, the teens all wanted to go to the Perry's house for the big meeting, but both parents were adamant about keeping the children out of it. Mr. Harris stressed again the seriousness of the matter – they had no way of knowing who was involved and if somebody was capable of such cruelty to an animal, there was no telling what else they might do. And, he warned, if criminal charges were pressed, any name even remotely associated with these accusations could become a target for vengeance. He was not going to allow the teens to get involved in any of this. He promised to pay attention to every word that was said and deliver a full report when they returned. His children knew he would deliver on his promise.

It was stressful for the adults. Mrs. Jackson had her doubts about the safety of marching into somebody's house and accusing them of animal abuse, even with Mr. Harris at her side. But Erin and Dakota and all of the Conroys had been guests at the Perry's for the regatta brunch and the Fourth of July party, so it wasn't like going to a total stranger's house. Mrs. Jackson's love of animals and her sense of justice helped her overcome her fears – if they didn't stand up for Harry, who would?

Mr. Harris assured her it would be a civilized meeting and he kept the few nagging doubts he had to himself. They had talked about bringing Harry with them, but decided against it. After all, they had plenty of evidence so they didn't need to drag the poor dog into this. Audrey had taken a ton of pictures of Harry for them and they had a copy of the bill from the vet with details about the dog's injuries. The vet was certain the injuries had come from a fight and had volunteered to testify if necessary.

In spite of all the reassurances they gave each other, both adults were nervous when they pulled into the winding driveway and parked in front of the imposing mansion. The impressive house and perfectly landscaped gardens were more than a little intimidating for such modest people, and to arrive in the pouring rain, surrounded by thunder and lightning, did not help their comfort level any. Mr. Harris and Mrs. Jackson exchanged grim smiles before they opened their car doors and ran to the house. They were surprised when Mr. Perry opened the door for them before they even rang the bell and ushered them inside.

"They should be there by now," said Erin with a worried look on her face. "I wonder how it's going."

"They can take care of themselves, Erin. Don't worry," Tommy reassured her. "You've never seen my Mom when she gets mad – I think Mr. Perry is the one you need to worry about!" Everybody laughed at his remark because it was incredibly easy for all of them to imagine Mrs. Jackson fighting to protect a dog, especially an injured one.

"I know they'll be OK," Erin said. "It's just such a terrible thing. Poor Harry! I can't wait to hear the story about what really happened to him."

"You know what, Erin?" Audrey asked with her hands on her hips, "This totally messes up our plans for Cody's party." She was trying to distract her friend by talking about something fun.

Dakota looked at the girls curiously, but didn't say anything.

"Yeah, I guess it does," said Erin thoughtfully, grateful to Audrey for changing the subject. "The twins are really the only people we know here who we could have invited."

"What about me?" asked Tommy with an exaggerated frown. "Don't I count?"

"You're almost like family," Audrey explained. "We wanted to surprise Dakota."

"I see what you mean," Dakota said thoughtfully. "I'm sure the twins won't want to have anything to do with us after today." He paused before opening his arms dramatically, "No big deal. As long as I spend my birthday with you guys – and Thomas Jefferson, of course - I'll be fine. Let's plan the party now."

Dakota was only kidding, but neither Tommy nor the girls picked up on his attempt at humor at first.

Audrey finally realized Dakota was teasing them, "That's actually not such a bad idea," she said as a smile slowly spread across her face. "It'll give us something to do to take our minds off Harry." She looked pleased with herself for thinking of this. "Your birthday's on a Monday, so you'll be working in the morning. Would you like to celebrate with Thomas Jefferson in the nineteenth century or should we plan your party for a weekend in the present?"

"I think the weekend sounds good. Then I get to have cake again on my birthday and sort of stretch it out to Monday," Dakota was starting to enjoy this. "I wonder how Thomas Jefferson celebrated his birthday...I know he was born on April 13, 1743. When do you think they started having birthday cakes? I need to research that..."

"I should have known better than to open this conversation to history," Audrey moaned. "Will I never learn?"

"What kind of cake would you like?" Erin asked her brother.

"When exactly is your birthday?" Tommy asked.

"Chocolate cake with chocolate frosting, August 10th, two weeks from tomorrow," answered Dakota quickly. "When's yours?"

Erin seemed really interested in Tommy's answer.

"Around Christmas," he said vaguely.

"When exactly around Christmas?" Erin pressured him.

"It's actually on Christmas Day," answered Tommy finally.

"Cool," said Audrey.

"I don't know about that," said Dakota. "I would think having your birthday on Christmas kind of stinks because you don't get as many presents."

"Yeah, but I bet nobody forgets your birthday," countered Audrey.

"It doesn't really matter 'cause I can't change it anyway," laughed Tommy. "I thought we were planning Dakota's party. Let's keep on track here, guys…"

They joked around for a while and actually did plan Dakota's birthday. Audrey had been right – it was a good distraction to talk about something besides Harry, at least for a little while. However, all conversation stopped the instant they heard the car in the driveway.

Chapter 19
Guilty

Later, Mr. Harris said he wished he had a picture of the faces lined up at the door when he and Mrs. Jackson returned from the Perry's. Even Sadie and Patches had sensed something was going on and pushed their way into the middle of the group on the porch, tails wagging.

"That was intense!" said Mrs. Jackson, shaking off her wet coat. "I guess I didn't realize how nervous I was until we got out of there."

"It was definitely interesting," Mr. Harris added.

"What happened?" chorused the teens.

"It went well. Everything's fine," reassured Mr. Harris.

"Mr. Perry is selling his dogs," explained Mrs. Jackson. "So we did save them! I'm so glad we went there." She turned to Mr. Harris, "Thank you, John. I think this worked out much better than if I had just gone to Animal Control on my own."

"Dad, tell us what happened," pleaded Dakota. "You promised to give us a detailed report!"

"Would you like some tea, Mrs. Jackson? Dad?" Erin asked politely.

"Thank you for asking, dear," said Mrs. Jackson. "Why don't I make us some tea while your father tells you the whole story – from the beginning."

"Okay, here goes," said Mr. Harris. He sat down in an armchair opposite the couch full of teenagers, obviously enjoying the suspense. *It must be the storyteller in him*, thought Erin.

"Mr. and Mrs. Perry were very polite. They were both in the living room when we arrived and there was another man there as well."

"Was the other man the dog trainer?" asked Erin.

"Were the twins there?" asked Audrey.

"Yes, the man was the trainer, and no, the twins were nowhere in sight," answered Mr. Harris, raising his eyebrow a little at the interruption. "After we all introduced ourselves, Mr. Perry explained who the trainer was. He got straight to the point."

"I couldn't believe it, but Mr. Perry assumed full responsibility before we even said a word," said Mr. Harris in a surprised voice and paused to allow his statement to sink in with his audience. "I can only assume that his wife told him what we came to talk about because he was ready for us. Mr. Perry confessed that his dogs had always been among his prize possessions, but he also admitted he only owned them for breeding and dog shows. He never considered them pets." When Erin started to say something, her father held his finger to his lips and silenced her before he continued, "He also clearly stated that it is no crime to own dogs solely for breeding and show purposes."

"We had to agree with him there, even though it's not how we feel," interjected Mrs. Jackson as she set a mug of tea in front of Mr. Harris and plopped down in the chair next to him.

"Then he said that even if he did consider the dogs to be possessions rather than pets, he still had certain responsibilities towards them, and this is where he found himself guilty. He said he had trusted Charles, the trainer, and that had been his mistake. Mr. Perry said he now believes Charles has been organizing dog fights for years – of course, without Mr. Perry's knowledge or consent. The trainer took complete advantage of the fact that the family spends very little time at their lake house and that nobody in the family really cares about the dogs."

"The trainer didn't even look like he felt bad," interrupted Mrs. Jackson with amazement. "I couldn't believe it! And he never said a word the whole time we were there."

"Mr. Perry admitted to having suspicions from time to time," continued Mr. Harris, "but the trainer always seemed to have some excuse or plausible explanation for the dogs' injuries. And of course, it was easy for Mr. Perry to ignore his suspicions as long as the dogs did well in shows, and on top of that he said he was always busy with work and his family." Mr. Harris sipped his tea, enjoying the rapt attention of his audience.

"One of the breeders Mr. Perry knows in the UK recently made comments about some of the injuries on the Perry's dogs," continued Mr. Harris, good to his word about giving a full report. "This breeder said he doubted the wounds came from normal training or dog handling, and he encouraged Mr. Perry to investigate the injuries, starting with his trainer. Well, that was only two weeks ago."

"He may not be a dog lover like we are, but Mr. Perry is a businessman, and probably an ethical person as well. I do not believe he intentionally allowed any of his animals to be hurt and I certainly did not get the impression he would knowingly be involved in any criminal activity. In fact, he started acting on the breeder's suspicions almost immediately, but he was away on business all last week and hasn't been able to gather any hard evidence yet." Mr. Harris paused again for another sip of tea.

"Anyway," he continued, "Mr. Perry fired the trainer on the spot, in our presence. The story we told him about Harry convinced him that something was definitely up with Charles, even if he couldn't prove it. He gave Charles the opportunity to confess, explaining that it might help him later if criminal charges were filed and he was found guilty, but the trainer didn't say a word. The man earned my respect – Mr. Perry I mean, not the trainer," added Mr. Harris quickly when he saw the shocked looks on the faces in the room. "He did the right thing."

"And he said he was going to sell the dogs immediately to the breeder in the UK," added Mrs. Jackson. "He said the man has been begging him for years to sell and it seems like now is the right time to do it."

"So did the trainer just walk out the door while you were there?" asked Tommy.

"Pretty much," answered Mr. Harris. "Mr. Perry wrote him a check on the spot and told him to pack up his things and leave. He told the man to his face he believed Charles was guilty of organizing dog fights, but that he felt obligated to pay him because he didn't have sufficient proof. He advised the so-called trainer to get as far away from Lake Bonita as possible and then he sent the butler with him to make sure the man left without damaging or stealing anything on the way."

"The trainer was stone-faced the whole time we were there," added Mrs. Jackson. "He just stood there with a defiant stance and never answered any questions. He didn't even try to defend himself – he just stuck the check in his pocket when it was handed to him and marched out of the living room without looking back. He gave me the creeps," she shuddered. "I'm glad he's gone from here. I hope he takes Mr. Perry's advice and goes far, far away."

"But what about Harry?" asked Erin. "Does Mr. Perry want him back so he can sell him, too?"

"We get to keep him, dear," answered Mrs. Jackson, smiling. "I have to agree with your father - Mr. Perry earned my respect today. Even though he talked about his dogs as if they were only an investment, he understood that we felt like Harry was a pet - our pet. He thanked us for taking care of Harry and insisted on giving me money for the vet bills. That was the last thing I expected to happen!"

"Did you see the twins at all?" asked Audrey.

"Not a sign of them," answered Mrs. Jackson, "but you could probably spend days in that big old house without seeing anyone. I've never seen anything like it, and it was beautifully decorated. I almost felt like asking Mrs. Perry for a tour of the house!" Mrs. Jackson laughed. "Wouldn't that have surprised her? She's already talking about what she'll do with the kennels after the dogs are gone – like they need more room in their summer house."

"Those kennels are bigger than our whole house, seriously," Erin added.

"Well, let this be a lesson for you - money can't buy everything," Mr. Harris simply could not resist an opportunity for a lecture. Erin and Dakota rolled their eyes at each other and shook their heads, grinning. They were used to it.

"I think this calls for a celebration," Dakota said, quickly changing the subject before his father got carried away with another full-blown parent lecture.

Erin followed her brother's lead. "I think the rain let up a little. Let's take these dogs for a walk."

Tommy and Audrey quickly joined Erin and Dakota on their way out the door, leaving the adults, or rather Mr. Harris, without an audience.

Mrs. Jackson stood up, too. "I really should be getting on home. The dogs need to be fed."

"Go ahead and take the car, Mom. I'll walk home later," Tommy told her.

Mr. Harris stood up when Mrs. Jackson did. "If you're not in a hurry, Amy, maybe this would be a good time for us to talk about...you know... the kids...you know..." Mr. Harris was actually at a loss for words.

"Do you mean talk about making arrangements for our children to visit each other after this summer?" Mrs. Jackson was very to-the-point.

"Yes," answered Mr. Harris quickly, grateful for her directness. He looked at his daughter, who turned beet red. Even Tommy looked a little embarrassed.

"Okay, Dad, we'll give you some space," said Dakota, taking the initiative and herding the whole group out the door with the dogs. "Don't be so self-conscious, Erin," he said to his sister on the way out. "It's a good thing they're talking about it, otherwise you'd never see Tommy again after we go back home. You should be glad."

"I guess you're right," Erin admitted. "It's just so embarrassing."

"I for one will gladly suffer a little embarrassment if it means I get to see you after this summer," said Tommy, squeezing her hand.

"Oh mushy," said Audrey, teasing. "Let's go check out the lake. We didn't have anybody on spy duty in the rain."

"Which means, if your theory is right, something really exciting must have happened because nobody was there to take pictures," Tommy teased right back.

"I think I like you better mushy than sarcastic," countered Audrey. Suddenly, she stopped dead in her tracks. "Look!" she exclaimed, pointing at the water. "What are they doing? Tommy, I can't believe you just said that and there they are!"

The others stopped to see what Audrey was pointing at it. The two old fishermen were hauling something up out of the water. It was impossible to see what they threw into their boat, but their behavior was obviously sneaky, even at a distance.

"See how they keep looking around? They're afraid of being caught," Audrey was still pointing. "I just don't believe I don't have my camera with me." She turned to Tommy, "And don't you dare say a word." Tommy grinned, but remained silent.

"That does it," said Dakota with determination. "From now on we have to take this spy duty seriously, and that means somebody is out here at all times, even in the rain."

"Actually," said Erin thoughtfully, "we probably only have to watch when it's raining. Look out there - there's nobody out on the lake except for those guys. Whenever other people are around those old guys never do anything except throw a line in the water and pretend to fish. It's when they think they're alone that we need to watch them."

"You're right, Erin" said Audrey with confidence. "That means we need to watch early in the morning and late in the day."

"And when it's raining," added Dakota, "and probably at night, too."

"I'll spy for a little while now," offered Erin. "It has to be better than listening to Dad and Mrs. Jackson talk about parental supervision." There was a smile on her face and bit of sarcasm in her voice when she said that.

"I'd stay with you, Erin, but I should get home and feed the dogs. Who knows how long Mom will be," Tommy really wanted to stay. "I'll come back after I'm done," he promised.

"Those guys definitely put something in their boat," said Audrey. "And I can't believe we missed it. I'll spy with you for a while, Erin" she added, "but I doubt we'll see anything now. Boats are already starting to come out on the lake. I guess everybody had enough of being cooped up because of the rain."

"Okay, if you guys want to stay out here for a while, I'll walk back with Tommy and take the dogs with me," Dakota said. "They've been in the house long enough, too. It'll be good for them to be outside for a while. It'll be good for all of us."

After the boys left, the girls stood quietly for a few minutes staring out across the water. Sure enough, as the lake filled up with boaters, one of the grumpy old men threw out a fishing line and the two men just sat there in the same spot like they always did. Both girls saw it at the same time and looked at each other as if to say, *See?*

That cracked them both up. "Feeling better?" asked Audrey.

Erin nodded and smiled at her friend.

Chapter 20

Surprise!

Spy duty became the teens' primary activity. They were wildly curious and determined to find out what was going on. The drama with the Perry family subsided and Harry was healing well under Mrs. Jackson's excellent care, so there was plenty of time to pursue the suspicious activity in the little fishing boat.

They soon realized they were seriously onto something. The grumpy old men sat in the exact same spot every day – not roughly the same spot or about the same spot – their boat was in *exactly* the same spot every day. The spies did not see any more unidentified objects being hauled up out of the lake, but they did see the fishermen out there at all hours from dawn to dusk, with very few breaks. They figured the grumpy old men were guarding something beneath the surface of the lake.

"How do we find out what's down there?" Erin asked. It was the day after Mrs. Jackson and Mr. Harris had discussed arrangements for Tommy and Erin to visit each other after the summer, and both teens were feeling pretty good about the outcome of their parents' conversation. It had been worth a little bit of embarrassment to know they would be able to see each other when Erin was back in Dunellon.

"Let's dive for it," said Tommy simply.

"How deep is the lake?" asked Audrey.

"Not so deep – somewhere between 20 and 30 feet in most spots. There's a real deep part by the rocks, but it's much shallower here," explained Tommy.

"I don't think any of us have ever been that far underwater," said Dakota cautiously. "Have you? Do you think you can dive there and reach bottom?"

"Sure," said Tommy confidently. "The main thing I'm worried about is the fishermen. They're mean and they're serious about whatever is down there. It's going to be hard to find a time to dive when they're not watching. My mother would kill me if I got in a fight or arrested because of some silly hunch we had."

"We could go out there at night," suggested Erin eagerly.

"There's a full moon on Wednesday," added Dakota. "That's only two days away."

"Of course, you would know exactly when there's a full moon," teased his sister.

"I have an underwater flashlight," said Tommy. "We'll need that no matter what time we dive. I won't be able to see anything 20 feet underwater, even in broad daylight."

"My camera's an underwater camera," said Audrey enthusiastically. "You could take pictures of whatever is down there. That way you wouldn't have to bring anything up to the surface, which might be difficult - and I guess it might even be considered stealing, now that I think about it. Cody, who owns stuff at the bottom of a lake, anyway? Do you know?"

Three pairs of eyes turned to Dakota.

"That's a very good question and no, I don't know the answer. I'll have to look it up." He looked at Tommy and said with a grin, "but I don't need to be a lawyer to know it's not against the law to take pictures. Let's do it."

"Won't it be dangerous to dive at night, Tommy? Are you absolutely sure you can do this?" Erin asked her questions with genuine concern.

"Yes, I'm sure," was all he said with a smile on his face, obviously trying not to be patronizing.

"Cool," said Audrey. "I say let's do it."

"Wednesday night it is, then," confirmed Dakota. "What else do we need Tommy?"

"Not much. The camera, the flashlight, some rope. I'll think about it. Will your father let us take the kayaks out at night?"

"It might take a little convincing, but as long as we promise to stick together and be careful, it should be fine." As an afterthought, Dakota added, "but I don't think we need to tell him exactly why we want to go out at night."

"Let's just tell him we want to be out on the lake because it's a full moon," Erin suggested. "He's always cool about stuff like that. He'll understand."

As soon as the words were out of her mouth, Erin's eyes opened wide and she looked quickly from Audrey to Dakota with a look that said *oh no!* The three of them had shared some rather extraordinary full moon experiences the previous winter.

"Well, be sure to tell your father there are no Indian girls involved," said Audrey laughing.

"And no archeologists, either," added Dakota.

"It's a long story - I'll explain later," Erin promised Tommy when she saw the questioning look he gave all three of his friends. There were some things Erin had not yet shared with Tommy, in spite of the wicked crush she had on him. She was afraid that telling him about her visions of an Indian girl from another century (which her brother and Audrey had also shared) might make him turn and run. It was a complicated story. Maybe when he visited her in Dunellon...

"Should I ask some of the guys to come?" Tommy asked. Audrey's nickname for Tommy's skateboarding friends, "the guys," had stuck. The girls still didn't even know one of them by name. "Most of them are great divers and we all grew up on this lake," Tommy added.

"It wouldn't be bad to have more than one diver, but I don't think it's such a good idea to have a whole group of people out there," Audrey said deliberately.

"We can always ask the guys to come if we decide to do another dive," Erin suggested.

"I guess you're right, just remember that I need someone to be in the water at the other end of a rope when I dive," Tommy explained. "But I agree we need to be discreet, at least for this first dive, and it's not easy for any of those guys to be quiet."

The others nodded their heads, laughing. Tommy's skateboarding friends were a pretty rough-and-tumble lot, but they were well liked by all.

"Okay, we've got plenty of time to get the kayaks rigged up," said Dakota eagerly. "You're the boss, Tommy. Tell us exactly what we need to do..."

Taking the kayaks out at night was a lot more fun than plain old spy duty. Of course, with just two boats for four people, it meant two of the teenagers would be in the water at any given time. Considering how hot and humid the nights had been, being in the water sounded pretty refreshing and would probably be a lot less work than paddling a kayak. As the diver, Tommy was an obvious choice for water duty, and as the girl who had a crush on the diver, Erin was the obvious second choice. Nobody was surprised when she volunteered.

Mr. Harris laughed when the kids told him they wanted to take the boats out at night. He had been expecting them to ask since the beginning of summer and he was surprised it had taken them this long. It was a great idea, he agreed, but he did have a few stipulations - they had to wear life jackets at all times, put lights on the front of the kayaks and carry a cell phone with them in case of emergency. Nothing the spies couldn't handle.

Dakota had the great idea to call Jamie, the kayak instructor, who gladly lent them some lights for the boats and two extra life jackets. They tied ropes to the kayaks so Tommy and Erin could be towed in the water while Dakota and Audrey paddled. Once Tommy went under for his dive with a rope tied around his waist, Erin would be responsible for the other end. It was his line of communication with the surface, Tommy explained to her, and it was very important. Erin took it seriously.

Wednesday came quickly. Tommy provided the gear for the actual dive, which they strapped into the back of the kayak Dakota would be paddling. Audrey made sure she charged her waterproof camera, providing Tommy with yet another opportunity to make jokes about her camera theory. The spies were ready long before dusk and it was sheer torture for all of them to wait until dark.

Erin tried to talk the others into a game of putt-putt or Liar's Dice to kill time, but everybody else wanted to just hang out on the dock and watch the sunset. Dakota tried again to get Sadie to jump into the water from the dock, which again provided good entertainment for a while. The big friendly dog was so eager to please, especially when there were treats involved, but in spite of all the cannonball jumps demonstrated by humans, she simply would not jump.   Either she didn't understand what Dakota wanted or she had too much sense to jump when there was a perfectly good grassy slope available for her to get into the water. As usual, Patches didn't participate in the training session, but she ran up and down the path to the house about a hundred times to show everybody how happy she was.

Finally, already exhausted from multiple catapults off the dock, the spies took the dogs up to the house for the night and told Mr. Harris they were heading out in the kayaks. Of course, he warned them to be careful and of course, they promised they would be. He guaranteed them he would be watching the lights on their boats (which he jokingly called "headlights") from the deck and they knew he meant it.   It wasn't until they were actually in the water that the spies let their excitement show.

"What do you think we'll find down there?" asked Erin seriously, holding onto a rope in the water behind Audrey's kayak.

"I don't know," answered Audrey, "but I can't wait to find out."

"All I can think of is buried treasure, like gold bullion on a sunken pirate ship," said Dakota. "I know that's so corny and I know there isn't any treasure chest down there, but I feel like there's something really exciting or else those men wouldn't be guarding it."

"Well, you're right about no treasure chest," said Tommy's voice from somewhere in the water behind Dakota's kayak. "This is a man-made lake, remember? It's only been around for about 50 years and I doubt a pirate has ever been anywhere near here."

"What was it before?" asked Audrey. "What's down there?"

"Mostly farmland, like you see all over Central Virginia," answered Tommy. "The developers planned this as a lake from the start. They built a dam after they bought the land and then let nature take its course."

"What do you mean, let nature take its course?" asked Audrey.

"Well, there are a lot of streams, natural ones that feed into this valley. When the dam was built, the valley became a basin and the streams filled it up within two years, just like planned," Tommy explained. "Once the lake was made, they opened a release valve at the dam to maintain the level – you know - for after heavy rains or snow melts."

"Cool," said Dakota. "I never thought about it, but it makes sense."

"So what's down there was originally farmland. Do you think the fishermen found an old plow, or what?" joked Audrey. They all laughed.

"It has to be something like that – something that wouldn't just dissolve under water. Maybe some family heirloom that belonged to a farmer," Erin followed her friend's lead.

"How about a graveyard?" contributed Dakota. "That would be way cool."

"Disgusting," said Audrey.

"I like your first idea better, Dakota," said Tommy good-naturedly. "A treasure chest would be perfect. I could use about a million dollars."

"Seriously, what could be down there?" Erin's question brought them full circle.

"I have no idea," answered Audrey. "But I hope we're about to find out."

They paddled in silence for the next few minutes. The fishermen's spot was right in front of the lake house, but they paddled around a bit for the benefit of Mr. Harris, who they were certain would be watching them, at least for a little while.

It was beautiful on the water at night. The full moon was low on the horizon and it cast an eerie light over the dark water. Every sound was amplified in the nighttime stillness, and each paddle stroke echoed over the lake as it hit the surface and sent drops of water flying off into the moonlight.

"It's like a fairy tale," said Erin quietly. The only response from the others was a wave of agreeing murmurs. After several minutes of allowing themselves to be mesmerized by the tranquil night scene, Dakota turned his kayak toward their real destination. Audrey followed without a word, and before they knew it they were at the dive site.

"What on earth is this?" Erin's voice echoed over the water much louder than she had intended, shattering the peacefulness of the moment. "Hey, Audrey, stop paddling for a minute. Actually, can you turn your boat around so I have some light? I need to look at something," Erin splashed around in the water, ignoring the chorus of questions being thrown at her.

Audrey turned her boat around so that her headlight illuminated Erin.

"Whoa! Not in my eyes please," Erin covered her face with her hands. "Point the boat to my right – your left. That's better," she dropped her hand from her face and the others could see her fumbling with something in the water. She still did not tell them what she was doing.

Finally, Tommy let go of his tow rope and swam over to her.

"What is it, Erin?" he asked curiously, treading water in front of her.

"Look at this," she said, tugging on his life jacket so he was close enough to see what she was holding in her hand.

"It's a leaf," he said.

"And look at this," Erin said again, putting her hand over his and guiding it along the thin length of fishing line attached to the leaf.

"It's moored to something at the bottom of the lake. It's a marker," Tommy sounded surprised, excited.

"And the leaf is plastic," Erin said. "This is the spot the fishermen guard. They used the leaf like a buoy to mark it."

"Erin found a marker," Tommy said just loudly enough for the others to hear. "This is the spot. There's something down there for sure." He swam back to the side of Dakota's kayak.

"I need my diving gear," he said as he undid the straps holding his snorkel and fins in the back of the boat. "Dakota, can you hold the flashlight? Thank you." Tommy was a natural leader and the others trusted him. Whenever he asked his friends to do something, they did it almost without hesitation. He quickly put his flippers on and swam back to Erin and the buoy with his mask and flashlight ready.

"OK, this part might be a little tricky," said Tommy seriously. "I need to follow the line attached to the fake leaf all the way to the bottom of the lake, but I can't pull on it very hard because it's not that strong and I don't want to break it. I'll use the flashlight, so hopefully I can partly see the line and partly feel it underwater. With any luck it will guide me to whatever it is we're looking for." He turned to face Erin in the dark. "I tied the rope around my waist. Here's the other end. You need to keep tension on the rope, but don't pull on it. Give me a couple of distinct tugs if you need me to come up for any reason." He waited for a nod of acknowledgment from Erin before continuing.

"I have a diving bag with me and I'll try to bring up whatever it is I find, or at least part of it. It would be good to recover something, but if it's too heavy, I'll tie it to the rope and Erin can pull it up," Tommy's instructions were very detailed. "Keep the boat lights pointed here so I know where to surface, OK? I don't want to hit one of the kayaks when I'm surfacing in the dark and already out of breath." He paused for a moment. "Any questions? OK then, wish me luck," he said, adjusting his mask for the dive.

"Hold your horses, there, Indiana Jones," said Audrey, reaching out to hand her camera to Tommy. "Aren't you forgetting something?"

They all saw a huge grin flash across Tommy's face in the moonlight. "Thank you, Audrey," he said, laughing. The young diver adjusted his face mask again, gave his friends a thumbs-up signal and disappeared beneath the surface of the water.

Erin found herself holding her breath while she waited for Tommy, and her hands gripped the rope like her life depended on it. Or maybe, like Tommy's life depended on it. She saw the light from his flashlight grow dimmer as he moved deeper underwater and after what seemed like an eternity, the light disappeared totally. All three teens on the surface waited silently, their eyes glued to the spot where Tommy had disappeared. It seemed like they sat on the still water in the moonlight for another eternity.

"What are you kids doing out here?" The gruff voice that shattered the night was so close to Erin she almost flew out of the water. It was all she could do to remember to hold onto the rope, but instinctively, she gave it two hard tugs to signal Tommy to come up. She saw the two grumpy old fishermen steering their boat directly for the lights of the kayaks and she suddenly realized they hadn't seen her in the water. They didn't even know she was there.

Audrey and Dakota almost flipped their kayaks when they heard the voice bellowing out of the darkness, but they were both quick thinkers with fast reactions. Dakota, protective big brother that he was, glanced over to make sure his sister was OK before he positioned his kayak between Audrey and the fishermen's boat. Once the two kayaks were side by side, Erin swam behind Audrey's boat as quietly as possible to avoid being spotted. She was still holding onto Tommy's rope.

"Who's there?" Dakota asked loudly, sounding much more confident than he actually was. The headlights on the kayaks gave off enough light for him to see exactly who it was, but the question was the first thing that came to his mind. Just as Erin had instinctively known to tug on the rope, her brother instinctively knew he had to stall these fishermen, at least until Tommy came back up.

"You kids get the hell out of here!" shouted a second gruff voice, waving a very strong flashlight.

Audrey coughed loudly and started shouting at the men like a hysterical teenage girl. "You have no right to tell us what to do. This is a public lake and we have just as much right to be here as anybody else!" She barely paused for a breath before she started screaming again, "What are you doing out here in the middle of the night? Why don't you guys get out of here? Leave us alone!"

At first Dakota thought Audrey had lost her mind, but he quickly realized she was trying to make enough noise to cover the sound of Tommy surfacing. Dakota half heard and half sensed Tommy coming up for air on the far side of Audrey's kayak, and it took incredible willpower on Dakota's part not to turn and look. He wanted to make sure Tommy was OK and he wanted to know what Tommy had found, but he did not want the fishermen to know Tommy was there.

"Go home," said the first man. "I oughtta call the police on you kids."

"That won't be necessary," said a third man's authoritative voice from shore. Mr. Harris was standing on the deck of the lake house pointing a feeble flashlight beam at the group gathered on the water. "I already called them. They should be here any minute."

Chapter 21

Waiting

"Dad!" shouted Erin and Dakota at the same time. Erin started waving her arms from the water so her father could see her, which meant the fishermen could see her, too.

"What the ...." Both fishermen expressed surprise at seeing the girl in the water. Then, as if on cue, both gruff shouts abruptly ended as a floodlight illuminated all three boats and every being in the little group on the water. To complete the picture, Sadie and Patches appeared on the shoreline, running back and forth, barking non-stop.

"Police! Stay where you are," ordered another authoritative voice from the shore, waving the intense floodlight. "There's a police boat on the way. Is anybody injured?"

It took the stunned group in the water a minute to avert their eyes from the bright light and answer.

"We're fine," Dakota spoke up first. Then he thought to confirm the well-being of the others.

"Erin, are you OK?" he asked.

"I'm good," came the prompt reply from his sister.

"Audrey?" questioned Dakota.

"Good."

"Tommy?"

"Great," he answered laughing.

Each time a voice spoke, the little light from Mr. Harris's flashlight and the overwhelming beam of light from the police spotlight searched the water until the speaker signaled they were OK.

The fishermen looked dumbfounded when Tommy spoke, revealing yet another teenager in the water. They had only seen two kayaks with two teenagers on the water up until now, and they were obviously surprised to discover the two others in the water. They had been surprised when Mr. Harris appeared on the deck of the lake house and again when the police appeared on shore. But the biggest surprise of all had to be when a police boat pulled up right next to their little fishing boat in the middle of the night. The officers on board shined a light on the fishermen and politely asked them to step out of their boat.

"There's something down there, Mr. Harris. I don't know what it is, but I saw something." Tommy was standing on the deck of the lake house with the other teens, the dogs, two police officers and Mr. Harris. The kids had just come out of the water. They had towels wrapped around their shoulders and all of them were talking at once, trying to explain to the adults why they had gone diving at night.

"Hold on a minute, everybody," said the police officer, "one at a time." He turned to Tommy, "Were you the one who dived?" The officer waited for Tommy's nod, "Okay you first, then."

"I saw something down there," Tommy repeated. "We need to go back," the boy was so serious nobody doubted him for a second. The only question was, what exactly had he seen?

Audrey started to say something, but the officer stopped her, "Don't worry," he said authoritatively, "you'll all have a chance to tell your version of the story."

Without saying another word, Audrey handed her camera to Tommy. He smiled at her gratefully, and turned back to the officer, "I took pictures," he said, passing the camera to the policeman.

The man in uniform took the camera from Tommy and started looking at the pictures. "Have you seen these yet?" he asked. Tommy shook his head no. "Is this your camera?" the officer asked. Tommy shook his head again. "I need to take it with me, at least until I get the pictures off it."

"It's my camera, sir," said Audrey respectfully. "Would it be possible for me to download those pictures on my computer before you take the chip? My computer's in the living room."

"I don't see why not," the officer said, "but you'll have to do it in my presence." He smiled, "Sorry, but that's procedure."

"Officer, could your procedure wait just a few minutes?" interrupted Mr. Harris. "I think your star witnesses would be better off in dry clothes."

"Of course. I'm sorry I didn't think of that myself," said the officer apologetically. "Take your time, guys." Then he turned to Mr. Harris, "Maybe you can get me started with names and a little background information."

"I'd be glad to," offered Mr. Harris. "Please go change," he instructed the teens, who were still hanging around. "Your story can wait five minutes – shoo!" He waved his hands at the reluctant kids until they left the deck, the girls heading upstairs and the boys downstairs to Dakota's dungeon. All four of them looked out onto the lake before they went into the house.

It was a long night.

The police were convinced the teens had discovered something when they saw the photos Tommy had taken and heard the stories about the odd behavior of the fishermen, so they put a guard at the dive site until daylight. An official police diving team would arrive in the morning to investigate and file a complete report. The officers took the fishermen to the police station for questioning, but released them without pressing charges, at least for the time being. However, they did advise the two old men not to leave town and not to have any contact whatsoever with the teens at the lake house.

The officers took statements from all of the teens in the presence of Mr. Harris and, of course, he backed the kids 100 percent. He realized they occasionally succumbed to their wild imaginations, but he knew they were smart, level-headed young adults most of the time, not flaky teenagers. The pictures Tommy had taken underwater, however vague, supported the teens' suspicions and lent credibility to their theory. Most of the photos were sideways or at an angle and all of them were blurry and dark, but a few of them revealed silhouettes of open boxes or crates with something unrecognizable in them. Everything was covered with a thick layer of silt and debris, which made the contents of the crates look like big lumps.

Tommy had taken several pictures underwater, from different angles, as soon as he realized there was something on the floor of the lake. He knew it was important not to disturb anything, but curiosity and a sense of urgency (perhaps because he was running out of breath) had prompted him to gently brush away the layer of silt on top of one of the lumps in one of the crates to see what was underneath. It felt like a bottle, he told the others, but in the picture it was impossible to see what it was. Tommy explained apologetically that it had been really hard to hold the camera steady while he was also trying to shine the light and tread water at the same time.

It was almost 1 AM when the police left, promising to be back the next day with their divers. Everybody in the lake house was exhausted, but much too excited to sleep. Dakota wanted to drive Tommy home, but Mr. Harris insisted on driving the boy himself so he could reassure Mrs. Jackson in person. Tommy had called his mother earlier to let her know he was alright and that he would be home late, but he hadn't told her what was going on. Mr. Harris felt like he owed the woman an explanation – if she was still awake.

Erin, Audrey and Dakota spent several minutes looking at the lights from the police boat shining on the lake when they took the dogs out one last time before bed. Audrey made a comment about how mad the grumpy old fishermen must have been and the others murmured their agreement, but they were all too tired to start a conversation. It was reassuring to know the police were looking into matters because it meant they wouldn't have to deal with the fishermen any more - and spy duty was over.

"I can't believe they used a plastic leaf to mark the spot," Erin said the next morning as they sat down to breakfast on the deck.

"I can't believe you didn't try to scoop that one up sooner. It would have sped things up a little," laughed Audrey, "you got just about every other leaf on the lake."

Everybody was up early in spite of the late night because they were excited about following the police investigation. So far, nothing had happened on the water, but they planned on staying put until something did.

"I don't want to go to work today," said Dakota. "Do you think I should call in sick?"

"Why don't you drive to Monticello and talk to your boss in person?" suggested his father. "I bet he'll give you the day off if you tell him what happened."

"Yeah, they're all about digging stuff up," encouraged Erin.

"Maybe you can work from home - you know, observe the police investigation and report back to Monticello with all the details like an investigative reporter," laughed Audrey.

"I'll go talk to my boss," said Dakota. "I haven't missed a day so far and it's not exactly like the place will go to ruin if the grass isn't mowed for one day." The others nodded their encouragement for his idea and his logic.

Tommy stuck his head around the corner of the house while Dakota was debating what to do. "Good morning," he said excitedly. "Anything happen yet?"

The others greeted him warmly.

"Nothing's going on down there," said Erin, smiling broadly as Tommy pulled a chair up next to her.

"Help yourself, Tommy," said Mr. Harris, gesturing to the bagels and doughnuts on the table. "I'll bring you a plate. I was getting up anyway to go watch the news." He went into the kitchen and brought a plate back for Tommy. "Erin, call me if anything happens," he said before heading into the house.

"I guess I'm outta here," said Dakota. "Wish me luck."

"You'll be back in no time," said Audrey encouragingly.

"I'll explain what that's all about," Erin promised Tommy when she saw the questioning look on his face.

Dakota left reluctantly amid a chorus of goodbyes, while his sister and friends lingered over breakfast on the deck. Almost as soon as Old Blue was out of the driveway, Erin caught a flash of something on the water. She stood up and pointed dramatically at the lake, "Look, the fishermen are out there!"

Audrey and Tommy followed Erin to the railing and they watched the familiar little fishing boat pull up alongside the police boat.

"What nerve," said Audrey.

"I would love to hear what they're saying," said Tommy.

"Dad, come back out here," shouted Erin.

Mr. Harris quickly joined the teens watching the exchange between the men in the two boats. Obviously, the police were not going to let anyone near the site, but the fishermen were persistent. One of the officers in the boat gestured repeatedly, clearly trying to direct the fishing boat away from the area. The fishermen responded ever so slowly, moving only far enough away to stop the police from chastising them. The grumpy old men parked themselves about 50 yards away from the police boat, watching every move at the site.

"Let's take the policemen some coffee," said Mr. Harris spontaneously.

"Let's take them breakfast, too," added Audrey, joining in the fun. "I'll put together a picnic basket."

Tommy headed for the stairs, "I'll get the boats in the water. Mr. Harris, are you OK in a kayak?"

"I'll do my best," Mr. Harris answered with a wry smile on his face. "I've been trying to avoid getting into one of those since our lesson." He jumped up to follow Tommy down to the dock and under his breath he muttered, "Good thing it's close to shore."

"I'll help Audrey," said Erin, heading for the kitchen.

"Too bad Cody's not here," said Audrey quietly, genuinely sorry for her friend. "I hope he doesn't miss too much."

The dogs knew something was up and they hesitated, torn between the kitchen, which meant food, and the lake, which meant swimming. Sadie and Patches stood at the top of the path leading down to the dock, waiting for a word of encouragement from Tommy. When it finally came, both dogs flew down the path towards the water, almost bowling over the boy and the man on the way.

Mr. Harris confessed his nervousness to Tommy while the two of them put the boats in the water, but the boy reassured him there was nothing to be nervous about. There was very little boat traffic on the lake and they would both be wearing life vests, so even if he capsized, a refreshing dip in the lake would be the only damage done. Tommy promised not to try any fancy stuff while Mr. Harris was with him.

The girls arrived almost as soon as the boats were in the water.

"That was quick," said Mr. Harris, eyeing the basket.

"Coffee, cream and sugar, water, donuts, bagels and cream cheese," explained Audrey.

"I guess we'll soon see if there's any truth to that stereotype," said Erin laughing.

The others looked at her for a minute with blank expressions on their faces. Suddenly, her father burst out laughing, "I get it – donuts, policemen. That's so corny I could have said it. You're a girl after my own heart, Erin." The silly joke took his mind off the fact he was about to get into a kayak.

Erin had packed the food in plastic bags and Audrey had found a flat rectangular basket, which fit perfectly into the well in the back of Tommy's kayak. When everything was bungeed in, Tommy helped Mr. Harris get into the other kayak without flipping it. The man looked relieved when he was finally settled in the boat with a paddle in his hand. The hardest thing about kayaking was getting in and out of the boat.

Erin and Audrey helped them push off before running back up the path to watch from the deck. Sadie and Patches must have thought the view was better from up there, too because they tore up the path ahead of the girls much the same way they had raced down to the water earlier. The two dogs sat at attention on the deck with the girls and observed what was happening on the lake.

It was definitely anticlimactic. The girls watched the kayaks approach the police boat and they could see the fishermen watching the kayaks as well. The fishermen's agitation was obvious, even from a distance, which the girls found amusing. Erin saw her father pull up next to the police boat and she was pleasantly surprised by how well he maneuvered his kayak. It put a smile on her face.

The police seemed much friendlier to Tommy and Mr. Harris than they had been to the fishermen, but the message they gave them was obviously the same. The officers accepted the picnic basket with smiles and nods and then directed the kayaks to leave the site. Tommy talked to one of the officers as long as he could, taking advantage of the situation, while Mr. Harris turned his boat around to leave. Tommy waved up to Erin and Audrey on the deck, which made the policemen and the fishermen look up at the deck, too. The officers waved to the girls and the policeman holding the basket raised it up as if to say thank you, but the fishermen just scowled.

Chapter 22

Buried Treasure

Dakota arrived back at the house just as his father and Tommy were pulling the boats out of the water. He had easily convinced his boss to give him the day off and now he was excited to hear what had happened at the lake in his absence, but it turned out the budding archeologist hadn't missed anything. In fact, he still had a lot of waiting ahead of him. Dakota could have gone to work and mowed the presidential lawn, played putt-putt afterwards, picked up a pizza on the way home and still had plenty of time to kill before anything happened at the dive site.

In spite of the fact that nothing was happening, no one at the house wanted to leave their post on the deck. Around noon they finally took turns making sandwiches, even though they could have all gone out for lunch because there was still nothing happening. It was two o'clock before the police dive boat arrived on the scene, and once the preparation for the dive actually started, it was fascinating to watch. A small crowd of onlookers had gathered on the lake to watch the proceedings, and the police gave them all the same strict instructions to keep their distance and let the divers do their work. Finally, the impatient audience saw the first diver roll backwards off the boat into the water. He was followed by a small crew of divers with lights and cameras and all kinds of equipment.

The fishermen stayed in their boat, watching every move at the site. Of course, no one left the deck of the lake house the whole time the divers were underwater, but they had to keep moving around to get a good view through the trees. The suspense was intense and it seemed like forever before the first diver surfaced.

Erin thought her brother was going to have a heart attack from sheer excitement when he saw the first diver's head pop up out of the water. The diver did not get out of the water, but he handed his camera up to one of the men in the boat and waited for the other divers to surface. Then all of the divers in the water gathered around the man in the boat with the camera, obviously discussing the pictures. None of the people watching could understand the exact words being said, but they could hear the excitement in the men's voices and they could sense the high energy level of the policemen.

The officer in the boat talked to someone on his radio before sending two divers back down with the camera. It seemed like another eternity before they resurfaced, one with a bag in his hand and the other with the camera, both of which were passed to the officer in the boat. The officer in charge placed the bag in a larger plastic bag and started giving directions to the team. Within minutes, the divers were placing buoys with police markers saying *DO NOT CROSS* in a large circle around the dive site. Everybody watching was curious, but nobody was as excited as Dakota.

"Dad, talk to them!" he said excitedly, waving his arms. "They have to let us know what they found!"

His father looked at him affectionately, "I'll do my best son," he said seriously. "I don't think the police in the boat will divulge information to anyone, but I'll call the station. The fact that you guys started this whole investigation should count for something." Mr. Harris watched his son's excitement and remembered how Dakota's mother had always said the boy was "talking Italian" when he got really enthusiastic and waved his arms around like that. *She would have been proud of him*, he thought.

The teens stayed at their post on the deck while Mr. Harris went inside to make his phone call. It looked like the dive boat was going to remain at the site. People and equipment were moved from the first police boat to the dive boat, and when they were done, the first boat headed for the boat ramp on the far side of the lake. Most of the onlookers left once they realized nothing more was going to happen, but of course the fishermen stayed put. If possible, it looked like the men were even more upset than before. The teens' curiosity was growing.

Dakota jumped up eagerly when his father reappeared on the deck.

"It looks like it's your lucky day, Dakota," said Mr. Harris with a big smile on his face. He paused before continuing, just so he could tease his son. The opportunity was too tempting for him to pass up.

"Dad! What is going on? Talk to me!" exploded the boy, and the other teens followed with a chorus of questions.

"What did they say?"

"What did they find?"

"Is it buried treasure?"

Mr. Harris gave in to the clamoring group.

"As expected, the police wouldn't tell me anything about what they found," he said, watching the disappointed looks on his listeners' faces. "But," he added with a dramatic flair, "they did tell me that everything they recovered was being taken straight to Monticello for further examination."

Dakota's eyes just about popped out of his head. "Let's go," he said quickly, motioning to the others. "I'm sure somebody there will tell me what's going on. I know all the archeologists." He bolted for the car, suddenly oblivious to everything and everybody around him.

"Hold on a minute, son," Mr. Harris stopped the boy in his tracks, "Remember, this is a police investigation and there is going to be a lot of protocol and red tape. Please don't forget that, and be sure you don't overstep your bounds because of your excitement. You know you tend to get carried away sometimes."

Dakota nodded in his father's direction and quickly resumed his beeline for the car. Mr. Harris looked after him, shaking his head. He was pretty sure the boy hadn't listened to a word he said.

Erin smiled at her father, "Don't worry, Dad. We'll keep an eye on him. He'll be fine."

"Thanks, sweetheart," said Mr. Harris. "Please be back by seven. I'll find something to put on the table for dinner." He gave his daughter a quick kiss on the cheek and said goodbye to the others as they ran out the door behind Dakota.

It turned out to be a great dinner because Tommy's mother made it. Mrs. Jackson had called the lake house after receiving an excited message from her son, which worried her because she couldn't understand a word of it. She listened while Mr. Harris explained what had happened, sharing what little information he had, and Mrs. Jackson spontaneously invited them all over for dinner so she could get the information firsthand from the kids. Mr. Harris gratefully accepted the invitation and called Erin to let her know they would be having dinner at the Jackson's.

Not wanting to arrive empty-handed, especially when he was bringing three hungry teenagers for dinner, Mr. Harris stopped on his way over to the Jackson's and picked up some ice cream and a huge bag of dog food, both of which he figured might come in handy in the Jackson home. He was right on both counts. He was helping her feed the lucky rescue dogs when the incredibly excited teenagers arrived.

Dakota's arms flew through the air as he told his father and Mrs. Jackson bits and pieces of what had happened at Monticello. The other teens let him talk, but they were clearly just as excited as he was. All of their faces were literally glowing with excitement.

"Dad, it *is* buried treasure!" blurted Dakota as soon as he saw his father. "At least for the archeologists. There's a bunch of wooden crates at the bottom of the lake filled with bottles and the lead archeologist says it looks like they belonged to Thomas Jefferson!" The boy paused for dramatic effect.

"The diver didn't want to disturb the site, but he decided to bring up something for them to examine, so he just brought up one bottle," he continued. "They're going to send a team of divers down to investigate and tag all of the crates and their contents. Who knows what else they'll find! This is going to take months." Dakota paused for a breath. "Dad, we can't leave here until we know what's going on – I mean, I'm right in the middle of all this at Monticello..."

"How do they know it belonged to Jefferson?" asked Mrs. Jackson.

The teens smiled at each other and gave Dakota the floor again. They wanted him to enjoy this moment.

"Because there was a letter in the bottle written by Thomas Jefferson!" Dakota answered triumphantly. "And the diver said there were dozens more at the bottom of the lake."

"How did they figure that out so quickly?" asked Mr. Harris. "They didn't just open the bottle and pull the letter out, did they? Don't they have to follow all kinds of procedures for archeological discoveries like this?"

"It was so cool, Dad. These guys know *everything* about Thomas Jefferson." Dakota's arms continued to fly through the air as he spoke. "Even they couldn't believe it. One of the archeologists recognized the bottle immediately - he knew they used to bottle wine at Monticello. So then the guy in charge scraped away a little bit of the dirt on the outside of the bottle and they took pictures. They used some special camera with a super intense flash that lit up the inside of the bottle, so they could see what was inside."

Dakota paused, enjoying telling the story almost as much as he had enjoyed experiencing it firsthand. It took the adults a few seconds to digest what the boy had just said. Once they understood what they had heard, they were eager to learn more.

"Well?" asked Mrs. Jackson and Mr. Harris impatiently at the same time.

"They took the pictures from the bottle and blew them up on a big screen and you could actually see a couple of words. They said the paper must be in great condition. The bottles were sealed with corks and wax and they still appear to be watertight, so it looks like the paper is probably still dry. The guys said the letter is in great shape. It's amazing."

"Tell them about the letters," encouraged Erin. "I think this is the coolest part." Everyone was waiting for Dakota to continue.

"Oh yeah," he said eagerly. "At Monticello, they have scanned everything Jefferson ever wrote into a database, so they took the picture of the letters they got from the bottle and did a search in the database to see if it matched anything. Guess what? It was a perfect match to part of a letter that Jefferson wrote to a freed slave." Dakota thoroughly enjoyed his role as storyteller.

"I mean an *exact* match," reiterated Dakota.

"The copy machine!" interjected Mr. Harris. "The letter was written on Jefferson's copy machine we saw at Monticello." He looked very proud of himself.

"Very good, Dad. You guessed it," said Dakota. "And they have Jefferson's copy in the archives at Monticello.

"They found all that out in such a short time?" asked Mrs. Jackson incredulously.

"Computers, Mom," said Tommy. "It was way cool the way they did it. I can see why Dakota likes this archeology stuff."

"They used some fancy software to try to match the letters from the bottle with the letters in the archives," Audrey explained. "It was amazing – it was like in a movie where they search a database for fingerprints."

"They said it will take months, maybe even years, to fully examine and classify everything that's at the bottom of the lake, but it really was cool to be there when they first discovered what it was – or what it most likely is," Erin corrected herself.

"Yeah, and when you combine the historical part of archeology with the technology, it's awesome. I got some great pictures. I was hooked immediately – I can't wait to tell my father. He'll never believe this." Audrey said with a huge smile on her face. Her father was as passionate about history as Dakota.

"I hope all that excitement made you hungry," said Mrs. Jackson. "Please go wash up while I get this roast on the table. You can tell us the rest over dinner."

The woman's urging set everybody in motion. It was crowded at the little Jackson table, but the kitchen was cozy, the food was great, and everybody was elated about the discovery. Mrs. Jackson dished up pork roast with rosemary, roasted rosemary potatoes and a red beet salad. It was a bit fancier than most of her guests had expected, but they all enjoyed it (actually they scarfed it down) and the cook reaped a ton of compliments for her efforts. It was the perfect end to an incredibly exciting day.

The teens cleared the table after dinner while Mr. Harris set out bowls for ice cream. He had a pretty good idea of what the kids liked, so none of them were surprised to see he had bought their favorite flavors. There was nothing better than ice cream to celebrate an archeological find.

Dakota's imagination ran wild. The boy was absolutely in heaven as his listeners sat attentively, spoons in hand, while he speculated about what else they were going to find at the bottom of the lake. Harry snored loudly the whole evening from his nest under the kitchen table.

Chapter 23

Details of the Dig and, oh yeah, a Birthday

Between the labs at Monticello and his observation points from the deck of the lake house, and sometimes from a kayak on the water, Dakota buried himself in the details of the underwater excavation. His world was perfect. He followed every aspect of the project as closely as he could, even to the extent that he totally forgot about his birthday.

Dakota's preoccupation (or was it an obsession?) with the archeological find made it easy for the others to plan a party for his birthday. Since they didn't really know many kids at the lake, and the idea for a surprise party with the twins and some of their friends had been scrapped, they were back to square one.

Erin and Audrey were on their way to talk to Heather about plans for Dakota's birthday when they ran into the twins. Ever since the Harry incident, the girls had been nervous about seeing the twins because they were afraid it would be an uncomfortable situation. So it was a bit awkward when they ran into them at the Country Store, but the encounter was much less uncomfortable than the girls had anticipated. The twins actually seemed pleased to see the girls, especially Audrey. *What a surprise*, thought Erin.

Daniel appeared to be his usual confident self as he approached the girls.

"Hi there," he said as if nothing bad had happened. "Haven't seen you two for a while. How's your summer coming along? Are you bored to tears in our sleepy little lake town?"

"We're not bored at all," Audrey answered. When she started to expand on her lack of boredom, Erin gave her a friendly nudge from behind that stopped her in mid-sentence.

"Harry's doing great!" blurted Erin enthusiastically to cover Audrey's abrupt silence. For some reason, Erin did not want to tell the twins about their involvement with the excavation at the bottom of Lake Bonita. It was big news in the small community, so she was certain the twins knew about it, but she didn't want to share all the details with the snooty boys. Audrey gave her friend a quizzical look, but remained silent. It was one of those situations where she just had to trust her friend.

"Good, I'm glad to hear it. Thanks for taking him, by the way," said David. He actually sounded sincere. "Dad sold all the dogs after Charles left, but I'm glad Harry's with you."

"He's not really with us," Erin explained. "He's at the Jackson's."

"What a mess that whole thing was," said Daniel in his familiar snooty voice. "It's impossible to get good help these days."

Erin's mouth dropped open. Daniel's remark sounded like a snobby old lady's line from an old movie, a very bad old movie. She suddenly felt sorry for the twins. They just didn't get it.

"When are you going back to school?" she asked to change the subject.

"Next week," replied Daniel, still sounding extremely bored.

"Well good luck if we don't see you again," said Audrey. "Thanks again for inviting us to your party."

"Good luck," echoed Erin, "and tell your parents thank you, too." She had no idea why she said that. Maybe it was because they fired the trainer. Maybe it was because she just wanted to get away from the twins. She offered a limp wave goodbye to the boys with their patronizing looks and headed to the back of the store to find Heather. Audrey was right behind her.

Heather's smiling face was a pleasant change for the girls after the condescending boys. It was even more pleasant for Erin to find Tommy there with his cousin. The boy's face lit up when he saw Erin, and the two of them immediately retreated into their own little world, ignoring everything and everybody around them. Heather and Audrey exchanged sympathetic smiles. They were getting used to being invisible.

"Hi guys," said Heather with her usual bubbly charm. "Want some ice cream? My treat," she added.

"Thanks, Heather," said Audrey with enthusiasm. "The usual for me, please." Neither Tommy nor Erin responded, so

Heather just ignored them and continued piling huge scoops of mint chocolate chip ice cream into a sugar cone while she talked to Audrey.

"I guess since you're the only one having ice cream, I'll make it a big one," joked Heather, rolling her eyes in the direction of Tommy and Erin.

Audrey devoted her full attention to the ice cream once it was handed to her, thanking Heather in between bites. It was another hot day, and even inside with the air conditioning, the ice cream started to melt quickly.

"It's going to be hot again tonight," said Audrey. "I'm so glad we're on the water, but I wish we had real air conditioning. It's great to be able to just jump in the lake, especially at night, but by the time we hike back up the path to the house, we're ready to get back in the water again. I never knew how much I liked air conditioning until I didn't have it."

"I know. I think I'm a real baby when it comes to being cool in the summer – and warm in the winter, too," Heather chatted easily to anybody about anything, a perfect match for Audrey. "Hey, did you guys decide what to do for Dakota's birthday?"

Tommy actually tore his attention away from Erin when he heard the question. "Mom wants to bake him a cake," he said eagerly. "And she said we could have a party at our house and invite the guys over. They like him. "

"What do you think, Audrey?" Tommy looked directly at Erin when he asked Audrey the question.

Erin's eyes remained glued to Tommy while Audrey answered.

"Sounds cool to me. I like the guys and they're the only people we know here to invite to a party." Audrey nodded to Tommy, "That's really nice of your Mom. Let's do it Monday night. If we have the party early, maybe we can actually pull off a surprise, especially if it's at your house. Erin can ask Cody to pick her up there or something."

"That should work," said Tommy. "Actually, I'll make sure it works," he added. Again, he looked directly at Erin when he spoke.

"Great," Erin beamed at Tommy. "It'll be fun to surprise Cody. But be warned, you guys know what he's going to talk about if he has an audience."

"That's OK," said Heather. "I think everybody's interested in the dig. I know my Mom is. She said one of those fishermen is the man who has been trying to buy that house you're renting. She thinks they wanted to steal all that stuff they found down there."

"Your Mom should come, too, Heather," said Erin. "She'd be good company for the adults. I know my Dad would love to hear about the fishermen. Actually, everybody probably would. We hardly know anything about them."

"Hey, speaking of adults, should we invite some of the archeologists from Monticello? You know Dakota would be thrilled." Tommy looked to the girls for support.

"Actually, I think that's a good idea," said Erin, giving Tommy one of her best smiles ever.

"I do too," replied Audrey quickly. "Let's see," she mused, "skateboarders, archeologists, parents, a couple of mushy teenagers and a kennel full of dogs. Sounds like quite a party." She burst out laughing and the others quickly joined in.

"The name of the slave was Elijah Jackson," stated the professor from Monticello to the group gathered in the Jackson's living room. The professor looked like a cartoon caricature of a mad scientist, which somehow seemed appropriate. Dakota's family and friends had pulled off the surprise for his birthday party, which turned out to be exactly what Audrey had anticipated. Actually, it was better than planned because the professor turned the evening into a Q and A about the archeological discovery at the bottom of the lake and everybody in his audience was intently curious about the subject. The man was a pretty good speaker, which meant it was a great party, and most importantly, perfect for Dakota's birthday.

"Many of Thomas Jefferson's slaves learned to read and write, but we don't have any real evidence that Jefferson himself educated his slaves. It appears that he did allow some slaves at Monticello to study with his grandchildren, but we still don't know a lot about that," explained the professor. "The letters we found at the bottom of Lake Bonita were written by Jefferson to a freed slave who owned a small farm of his own. We know this because we have copies of these letters in our archives at Monticello." The professor explained Jefferson's copy machine to the group.

"Jefferson often corresponded with neighboring farmers about many aspects of farm life, not just crops, and at the time he was interested in the canning process, which he had seen and studied a bit in France. Canning was the subject of the first letter we found."

"Then why were the letters in bottles instead of cans?" This question came from one of the skateboarders.

"Good question," complimented the professor. "This letter belonged to Elijah Jackson, who we believe is responsible for preserving the letters in bottles. Mr. Jackson was not at all familiar with the canning process – he was simply the recipient of Mr. Jefferson's letter on the subject. Apparently, Mr. Jackson or someone in his household was quite adept at sealing bottles with cork and wax, the most common method of preserving anything in the late 1700's. This person may have learned these skills at Jefferson's vineyard. We still don't know who preserved the letters, but I for one am grateful that somebody valued the letters enough at the time to go to such lengths."

"My last name is Jackson," said Tommy. "Could we be related to Elijah Jackson?"

"That is unlikely young man, but your question does raise an interesting point," answered the professor slowly. "Most slaves took the surname of their owners, so it is possible Elijah was freed by one of your ancestors."

"Does that mean the Jackson family, whoever they are, owns the letters, or has a legal right to them?" This came from Mr. Harris.

"I think I can answer that," piped up a voice from the back of the room. Heather's mother seemed a little surprised at the sound of her own voice. "I'm a realtor," she explained, looking around the room. "Lots of people who have houses here are curious about stuff they find at the bottom of the lake, so I've done quite a bit of research on the subject. There are lots of legal terms like 'plats' and 'riparian rights' that I don't think we need to get into here, but the law is pretty straightforward and I think I can sum it up for you." She paused for a breath, looking around the room.

"Because this is a man-made lake, everything under water belongs to the lake owners' association. They built the lake and nothing in it belongs to individual homeowners. It used to be that property lines extended some distance into the middle of a body of water, but that law was changed several years ago." She paused a little self-consciously before making a final statement, "I am fairly certain the owners' association is aware of this law."

"Thank you. That was very well put," complimented the professor. "I believe you are correct, but my knowledge of the legal aspects of this archeological discovery is rather limited. However, that being said, I do believe the Monticello Foundation recently received a very generous donation from the Lake Bonita Association."

The audience applauded and the professor paused. He invited Dakota to join him before he started speaking again.

"I understand this young man is one of the teenagers credited with this amazing discovery. We owe all of these young people a great deal of thanks." The professor put his arm around Dakota's shoulders. "I consider it my good fortune to have worked with him this summer. Happy Birthday, Dakota."

The little living room erupted in applause again. Dakota beamed, and so did his father, his sister, and all of "the guys." Everybody was happy for him. Mrs. Jackson marched into the living room carrying a cake blazing with 17 candles and the applause turned into a pretty good chorus of "Happy Birthday." Dakota smiled at the professor, oblivious to all the attention from the others. Finally, the professor gave him a gentle nudge, urging him to speak.

Erin and Audrey exchanged huge grins and "oh no" looks, both of them anticipating a long rambling speech from the birthday boy, but he surprised them both.

Dakota blew out the candles amid much laughter and cheering and then stood silent for a moment, still beaming. He looked around the room and said, "Thank you – all of you. This is the best birthday I could have ever imagined. Now, let's eat that cake!"

Chapter 24

Signs and Promises

"Did you know that Thomas Jefferson loved ice cream?" asked Tommy. He and Dakota were sitting on the dock dangling their feet in the water while they threw sticks out into the lake in a final, desperate attempt to get Sadie to jump. The dog stood between them, wagging her tail happily with all four feet firmly planted. She was not about to jump anywhere. Patches ran up and down the path to the house trying to decide where she really wanted to be.

"How do you know that?" asked Dakota.

"I researched it," said Tommy proudly. "He had an ice house and he harvested ice from the river and made ice cream all summer long."

"What was his favorite flavor?" asked Dakota.

"No idea," answered Tommy promptly. "I didn't do that much research."

Both boys burst out laughing and looked up towards the house with anticipation. It was the last day at the lake house for Erin, Audrey and Dakota, and it was going to be hard to say goodbye, especially for Erin and Tommy. Both parents had assured their kids they would be able to visit each other, but it was hard to imagine their future as clearly as the summer days on the lake.

If it weren't for the fact they were leaving, it would have been a perfect day. Erin, Audrey and Dakota had headed into the nature preserve early enough to hear the morning birds and watch a fine mist burn off the lake, hoping to see Lucy one last time. Erin had memories and plenty of pictures, thanks to Audrey, but saying a final goodbye to the albino really meant something to her. Audrey hoped desperately that Lucy would appear for her friend's sake because this was going to be a really rough day for Erin. Seeing the albino might make all the difference to her – like a sign of hope.

They met Tommy at the usual spot in the woods. Erin almost burst into tears when she saw him, but he shook his head and smiled at her, motioning them all to silence by putting a finger to his lips. Tommy took Erin's hand with a beautiful smile still on his face and led the silent group back down the path where he had just been. They hadn't gone more than 50 feet when Tommy stopped and pointed off into the woods on his right. Lying in a clearing, looking like magic, were two albino deer. Two!

Erin had a smile on her face the whole way home, but there was more than a trace of sadness in her eyes.

The boys were banished from the house along with the dogs while the girls finished packing and cleaning up. All of the stuff that was leaving the lake house was piled in the driveway and Mr. Harris was loading the van *his* way. Dakota was going to drive Old Blue back to Dunellon, with strict instructions to follow his father carefully. The teens had convinced Mr. Harris to leave as late as possible, which hadn't really been all that difficult. He was going to miss this house, too.

"When do you think you'll come visit us?" asked Dakota seriously.

"I doubt it will be before Thanksgiving," answered Tommy. "And even then, it's not fair to leave Mom alone for long, especially with all those dogs." He was sad. "You guys could come here though – like next weekend, right?"

Both boys laughed too loudly and the seriousness of the moment passed, but there was still an undercurrent of sadness in the air between them. Dakota was trying to get Sadie to jump again when they saw Mr. Harris tearing down the path to the dock waving a newspaper in his hand and calling their names. The boys watched the man make his way down to the dock, wondering what on earth would possibly make the serious, sedate author act like a teenage boy. Even Sadie tilted her head and looked puzzled. Everybody on the dock watched as Patches tore up the path to meet the man and then ran back down with him.

By the time Mr. Harris reached the boys, the girls were running down the path to see what all the commotion was about.

"Wait for us!" shouted Erin. Patches ran back up to meet the girls and ran back down with them. She liked this.

"Look at this," exclaimed Mr. Harris, completely out of breath. "You made the front page of the paper!" They all crowded around the man holding the newspaper, but nobody could read anything because of all the jostling around.

"Dad, read it out loud to us," said Erin as she plopped down in a chair. Tommy quickly sat down next to her.

Mr. Harris took a few deep breaths and tried to hold the paper still. "'Thanks to the diligent efforts of a group of local teens, the Monticello Foundation has been able to retrieve a unique collection of letters written by President Thomas Jefferson almost 200 years ago.'" Mr. Harris read the entire article to his eager audience. It talked about the local boy, Tommy Jackson, and the possibility that the slave who had preserved the letters had been freed by Tommy's ancestors, and it mentioned the girls from Dunellon, but most of the article was about the teenage boy who had a summer job at Monticello and was so passionate about archeology and history. The author of the article had obviously talked to the professors at Monticello.

"What about the fishermen?" asked Erin. "Does it say anything about them?"

"Let's see," said Mr. Harris. "Here it is at the bottom of the article. 'Two area residents have been charged with attempted theft of property belonging to the Lake Bonita

Homeowners' Association. Police are still unsure about the exact nature of the involvement of the two men and the matter is currently under investigation. Both men have been released on bail and ordered not to leave the state. Reliable sources report that the police uncovered evidence in a fishing boat belonging to one of the men, which links them to the discovery of the letters. The boat has been impounded.'"

"They should have been charged with several counts of meanness..." Erin quipped.

"Listen to this," continued Mr. Harris, even more excited than before. "'As a token of their gratitude, the Monticello Foundation has elected to grant each of the four teens a $10,000 scholarship to the college of their choice. The Foundation believes it would never have seen the letters if not for the vigilance of these young heroes. The scholarships are intended to encourage higher learning, hopefully in the field of archeology. '"

It took a minute for the full effect of the news to sink in, and when it did the dock rocked with excitement. The scholarships would make a difference in the lives of all the teens, but it was especially important for Dakota, Erin and Tommy. Mr. Harris hugged each one of the excited heroes in turn, and the boys crowned the little celebration by cannonballing into the lake.

"I have to call my mother," said Tommy, climbing out of the water. "She'll be thrilled."

"I'll go up to the house with you," Erin said eagerly. "I need to finish getting our picnic ready."

"Yeah, I'm going too," chimed in Dakota. "I need a towel. Are they packed already, Erin?"

"Hey Cody, stay here for a minute," said Audrey quickly, grabbing his arm to hold him back. Under her breath, she said quietly, "Let them a have a few minutes alone to say goodbye."

Audrey watched the blank expression on Dakota's face turn to one of understanding, and she burst out laughing.

"OK, I get it," he said. "Let's read that article again. I want to know who wrote it."

Tommy held Erin's hand tightly on the walk up to the house. They had talked a lot about saying goodbye at the end of the summer and they knew it was going to happen, but somehow it was very different now that the time had really come. Erin was incredibly sad, but at the same time she kept telling herself not to be sad because she was still with Tommy. She would have plenty of time to be sad when she was back in Dunellon – without him.

When they reached the deck, out of sight from the others below, Erin turned to face Tommy. She wanted to tell him all the wild thoughts running through her head and how it had been the best summer of her life and how much she was going to miss him, but as soon as she opened her mouth to speak, he put his finger on her lips and shook his head.

"Erin, please don't say anything," he said quietly. "Don't you think we've talked about this enough?"

She nodded slowly, without saying a word.

"I have something for you," Tommy said. He pulled a small box out of his pocket and handed it to her. "Open it," he said softly.

Erin's eyes filled with tears as she opened the small box and saw a gold heart-shaped locket.

"It has pictures inside," said Tommy with a smile on his face.

Erin fumbled with the locket and burst into tears when she opened it. Inside were two small photographs on either side of the heart – one of Lucy and one of Tommy and Harry.

Tommy smiled and gently put the necklace around Erin's neck, sending electricity through her entire body when his fingers touched her skin. Then he lifted her chin, looked straight into her eyes and kissed her softly on the lips.

Erin's world exploded. His lips were warm and soft and she felt his hand on the back of her head for a brief moment before his arms wrapped around her. She melted and sighed. She was thrilled and sad and happy and a little scared and she never wanted the moment to end.

When the kiss finally did end, Tommy pulled his head away from Erin just far enough so he could speak. Erin stared at her feet – and at Tommy's feet so close to hers.

"I'm going to miss you so much," he said. "But remember this – the only reason it's so hard to leave is because what we have is so special. We wouldn't be sad if we had never met. Would you rather not have met at all?"

"I'll be fine. Don't worry about me. But I am going to miss you," Erin hugged him tightly before she pulled away. "Let me get this picnic together. Weren't you going to call your Mom?" She busied herself with plates of food, trying not to cry in front of Tommy.

It took Tommy a minute to understand why she had pulled away from him, but once he did, he smiled at her and followed her lead. He helped carry food out to the deck, making small talk about how much the scholarship meant to him and how he had developed a new-found interest in archeology. He never did call his mother.

When Erin called the rest of the group up from the water for lunch, they all sat on the deck for one last time and looked out at the expanse of lake below them. An area was still cordoned off with police tape, but the boats had been replaced by a platform with a video camera and signs explaining that this was a Monticello Foundation research area and off limits to the general public. There was heavy netting that extended all the way from the platform on the surface of the water down to the bottom of the lake.

In an effort to distract his sister from her impending gloom, Dakota made wisecracks about the food on the table. It really was a "clean out the fridge" meal, literally a pickles and ice cream lunch. Nobody seemed too interested in Dakota's corny jokes and nobody seemed too interested in the food, either. They were all staring at the water, each of them lost in their own thoughts, when they heard voices from the front of the house.

"We're on the deck – come on out back," said Mr. Harris loudly.

"I'm glad I caught you," said Mrs. Jackson as she came around the corner. "I wanted to say goodbye and I brought you some cookies for the drive home."

Heather's face appeared right behind her. "I wanted to say goodbye, too," the girl said with her usual friendly enthusiasm. "Mom said you're welcome to stay with us anytime you come back. I guess if there's not enough room at Tommy's for all of you..."

The arrival of the visitors signaled the end of lunch and pretty soon everybody was in motion. The girls finished cleaning up the kitchen and sent Dakota out with the last of the trash. Time was running out. Mrs. Jackson and Heather gave everybody warm hugs and made them all promise to come back to Lake Bonita.

"You should see it in the winter," said Heather. "It's beautiful."

"And quiet, too. Hardly any tourists come when it's cold," said Tommy, looking at Mr. Harris. "It would be perfect for writing."

Mr. Harris smiled and made a little speech about what a great summer it had been. He went on about how much he had enjoyed meeting everyone and how Tommy was welcome anytime in Dunellon, and then he announced that it was time to go. The little group slowly headed out to the cars with the cookies and the dogs while Mr. Harris locked the house one last time.

"Where's the newspaper article?" asked Mr. Harris. "That's one I'd like to keep."

"I think I left it on the dock," said Dakota. "I'll go get it." He started down the path with Sadie and Patches at his heels. The two dogs were determined not to miss a thing. When he reached the dock, Dakota picked up the newspaper and turned to face the others in the driveway, waving the paper in his hand while Sadie watched him eagerly. On impulse, Dakota pretended to throw the newspaper into the lake.

"Fetch, Sadie, fetch!" he said loudly, grinning at the dog.

Sadie looked at Dakota and hesitated for just a fraction of a second before she took a flying leap off the dock, splashing loudly as she hit the water with her tail wagging and her head held high.

The End

7448096R0

Made in the USA
Charleston, SC
05 March 2011